THE VOICE
IN MY EAR

THE VOICE IN MY EAR

Frances Leviston

JONATHAN CAPE

LONDON

1 3 5 7 9 10 8 6 4 2

Jonathan Cape, an imprint of Vintage,
20 Vauxhall Bridge Road,
London SW1V 2SA

Jonathan Cape is part of the Penguin Random House group of companies
whose addresses can be found at global.penguinrandomhouse.com.

Penguin
Random House
UK

First published by Jonathan Cape in 2020

penguin.co.uk/vintage

A CIP catalogue record for this book is available from the British Library

ISBN 9781787331983

Typeset in 11.75/17 pt Bembo Std
by Integra Software Services Pvt. Ltd, Pondicherry

Printed and bound in Great Britain by Clays Ltd, Elcograf S.p.A.

Penguin Random House is committed to a sustainable future for our
business, our readers and our planet. This book is made from
Forest Stewardship Council® certified paper.

For Paul

CONTENTS

THE VOICE IN MY EAR   1

BRODERIE ANGLAISE   11

PATIENCE   29

THE MAN IN ROOM SIX   79

WITH THEM INTERCEDE
FOR US ALL   89

WOULD YOU RATHER   113

MUSTER'S PUPPETS
PRESENTS ...   131

A SOURCE   161

PLIGHT   175

NO TWO WERE E'ER WED   203

ACKNOWLEDGEMENTS   261

THE VOICE IN MY EAR

The first production team have gone to an awards ceremony in King's Cross, the anchor to the Portland with foetal distress. This is Claire's big break. She takes her mark, and feels the hiss of the open channel flood her head.

—*Sixty seconds.*

Sprayed ends of hair shine and shake in her peripheral vision. A soft brush whisks across her nose, a roller across her lapels. The earpiece feeds her the end of the buffering ads, Maybelline and Dolmio, then a trailer for a costume drama, before the continuity announcer begins: 'And now, standing in ...'

—*Ten seconds to air. Eight. Seven.*

Her hands are cold, her feet on another planet. She looks squarely down the autocue and reads, 'GOOD EVENING. I'M CLAIRE ASHBY.

'TONIGHT: AS CONSPIRACY CHARGES AGAINST FORMER GOVERNMENT COMMUNICATIONS DIRECTORS ARE UPHELD AT

THE COURT OF APPEALS, WE ASK WHICH OF THE SUTHERLAND ENQUIRY'S RECOMMENDATIONS HAVE BEEN IMPLEMENTED, AND WHAT THIS MEANS FOR THE FREEDOM OF THE PRESS.

'BUT FIRST: RELIEF AS THE LONGEST AND MOST EXPENSIVE STRIKE IN SOUTH AFRICAN HISTORY COMES TO AN END — FOR NOW — WITH A DEAL PROMISING PLATINUM MINERS A THREE THOUSAND RAND PAY RAISE OVER THREE YEARS. BUT AT WHAT COST TO LONG-TERM JOB SECURITY, AND WHAT COST TO THE ANC?'

She pictures the white Meccano rigging and dove-coloured silos of the Anglo-American platinum mine on the B-roll that is now being cued. She cut it herself that morning.

'Almost two years ago,' the voiceover begins, 'this mine in Marikana ...'

Her ears pop. She wiggles her toes inside the hard shoes. She's done it, the first bit, and now she is huge and triumphant, a carnival queen on her float of light.

—*New positions. Camera three ready.*

The next angle jumps up on the monitor. She watches herself enter the frame and settle behind the desk. Now the studio guests come in, stepping over cables, broaching the circle of lights. The first of them, a woman, only four or five years older than Claire, tall and heavy-bosomed in a tailored blue dress, offers a handshake that is nothing more than a touch of palms, then sits and stares up at the rig. Some kind of childish torpor keeps forcing her to smother huge yawns.

'Look at Claire,' says the woman acting up as floor manager. 'Look at each other. Don't look down the camera, just pretend it's not there.'

The male guest is wearing a shirt in a mushy colour, bad for TV. He clasps Claire's hand in a damp grip and says, 'You must be as nervous as me. I mean – I don't mean ...'

Sweat glistens on his forehead. The make-up girl powders it away, obliterating freckles, revealing that without them his face does not make sense. The woman in the blue dress refuses to be powdered: just refuses, with the flat of her hand. Her skin is so clear and dewy that Claire wonders if she's pregnant.

A crackle. —*Back to you in ten, nine, eight ...*

On the screen Claire sees the school photo looming behind her shoulder, long face, red hair. She pokes the earpiece, then straightens up and sets her shoulders as the text begins to scroll.

'THE DEATH OF TEENAGER BEVERLEY PARKER HAS LED TO RENEWED CALLS FOR THE SOCIAL MEDIA ACTIVITIES OF ADULTS WHO WORK WITH CHILDREN TO BE MORE CLOSELY REGULATED. BEVERLEY TOOK HER OWN LIFE LAST FRIDAY AT HER FAMILY HOME IN BIRMINGHAM, JUST THREE MONTHS AFTER THE CONVICTION OF HER FORMER PHYSICS TEACHER NEAL RICHARDS ON CHARGES OF SEXUAL ACTIVITY WITH A CHILD. IT WAS REVEALED DURING THE TRIAL THAT IN ADDITION TO HAVING SEX WITH THE FIFTEEN-YEAR-OLD ON MULTIPLE OCCASIONS, RICHARDS HAD BEEN SENDING HER UP TO A DOZEN MESSAGES A DAY VIA TEXT AND ON SOCIAL MEDIA WEBSITES. THE COUPLE CONTINUED TO WRITE LETTERS TO EACH OTHER EVEN AFTER HE HAD BEEN ARRESTED.

'CAROLINE LOVELL,' Claire says, turning to the woman in the blue dress, 'your organisation Mothers of the Innocent has been one of the loudest voices calling for increased regulation. What exactly do you want to see happen?'

As if she runs purely off the energy of live television, Caroline springs to life, all lassitude gone.

'What we *don't* want to see,' she says, 'are any more cases like the tragic case of Beverley Parker, a young girl taken advantage of systematically by her teacher over a number of months, a shocking sequence of events, which has now ended with young Beverley taking her own life. What we are proposing is that schools insist on all contact between teachers and pupils taking place through school systems *only*, where it can be properly tracked—'

'That isn't the case already?'

'No, it's not, not clearly enough. Everyone *agrees* that social media contact with pupils isn't a good idea, but teachers are simply trusted to use their own judgement. What we want to see, and what we believe the British public would like to see, are much clearer boundaries about what's appropriate, so that everyone knows right from wrong—'

'But Richards *did* know it was wrong,' Claire says, glancing at her notes, 'he admitted as much in court, so how would that—'

'Boundaries don't exist simply for *criminals,* they exist for *victims*, too: they help victims know that what's happening is unacceptable. We want *all* pupils to be aware that social media is off limits. When I talk to people about this, most of them can't believe the law hasn't already taken a firmer stance.'

'Rob Dowling,' Claire says, 'is Caroline Lovell right? Does the British Teaching Association agree that we need more regulation?'

Rob is already nodding. 'The issues Caroline's raising are very important, and of course we must do everything we can to ensure that teachers *do* know the boundaries, that they *respect* the boundaries, especially on social media—'

'You should be doing that already,' Caroline says.

'Well, if you just listen—'

'—I *am* listening—'

'—you'll know that *is* what we're doing, and we won't stop looking for ways to improve teacher training, but the fact is—'

'The fact is not enough care is taken to make sure girls like Beverley aren't *exploited*—'

'Let me assure you,' Rob says, flushing, 'a great *deal* of care is taken. The vast majority of teachers are decent people, responsible, caring people, who absolutely know the difference between right and wrong, and are doing their best to deal with, not just the dangers, but also the *opportunities* new technology has created. Educators cannot be held *solely* responsible for these kinds—'

'Who else do we blame? The pupils?'

'Absolutely not, but there *are* other factors in play.'

'Such as what?' asks Claire.

'We all know,' Rob says, turning gratefully towards her, 'that teachers are chronically overworked and underpaid. What we need are more realistic workloads that would ensure all pupils receive the *right kind* of attention. The answer isn't to force more regulation on teachers, to give them yet another thing to feel anxious about, but instead to trust teachers to—'

'*Trust* them?' Caroline says. 'I'm sorry, but Neal Richards was trusted, and look what he did with *that*. Trust is the problem here. You have to recognise the special position you occupy, and accept that there simply *has* to be a greater burden of accountability because of—'

'—but that doesn't benefit the *pupils*—'

'It would have benefited Beverley Parker. It would have benefited Beverley's parents, who are grieving the loss of their daughter, and are actually now pressing for manslaughter charges against Neal Richards, that's how completely they feel he betrayed the trust placed in *him*.'

This is what pundits require, Claire thinks: absolute belief in whatever they are saying, even from a standing start. The marvellous capacity to self-convince. No one masters such a role cynically, despite what people think. Cynicism can be pried up around the edges. Only the faithful endure.

'And what *about* parents?' she asks. 'Since you've raised them. Where do they come in?'

'Claire,' says Caroline, swivelling towards her, 'the parents I represent for Mothers of the Innocent – and they're not just mothers, by the way, they're loving fathers as well – these parents are *extremely* concerned—'

'Everyone's *concerned*. But what responsibility do parents have for ensuring this kind of thing doesn't happen to their child?'

'Well, I'm not sure I understand the question, because I don't see how parents are in any way to blame for the fact that *paedophiles* and *abusers* get into the education—'

'No, we can't blame parents for that,' Claire says, 'they've got nothing to do with hiring teachers—'

'Parents are *not* to blame,' Rob nods.

'—but still they must bear *some* responsibility, mustn't they, as parents, somewhere along the line? Isn't that what parents are for?'

'I don't see your logic,' Caroline says. 'If I take my child to the zoo, and she gets mauled by a tiger, is that my fault? No, it's not my fault: it's the zoo's fault, it's the zookeeper's fault. That's just common sense.'

'Yes,' Rob says, 'and let's keep in mind here, the tragic exploitation of this young girl was a freak occurrence, and is *not*—'

'But Caroline,' Claire says, 'your zoo metaphor, how does it apply in this case? Because we've been told several times, by the school, by the media, even by you, that Beverley was a vulnerable young girl, that she was preyed upon *because* she was vulnerable – because of something in her personality or her circumstances, something about *her* – and that's not what tigers do, is it?'

'Tigers,' Caroline says, 'and obviously that's a metaphor, tigers are *predators*, they eat babies' – Rob nods vigorously at this – 'they attack babies and young children, not adults who can fend for themselves—'

'Well, I'm not sure that's true,' says Claire, 'but even so, that would be based on physical size, not psychological issues,

7

wouldn't it? And yet Beverley was emotionally vulnerable, you've said, psychologically vulnerable—'

'Yes—'

—*Stay on topic. You're wandering off.*

'—and you said her vulnerability had something to do with the situation in which she found herself—'

'Yes,' Caroline says, 'generally we find it's the vulnerable children, the isolated girls, that abusers are drawn towards. Schools should be doing more—'

'So they're vulnerable, they're isolated' – Claire is counting off the points on her fingers – 'they're maybe less aware of boundaries than other children, they maybe have fewer people to confide in—'

'Yes, that's right, that's what we tend to find—'

'—and yet you want me to believe that parents bear no responsibility at all for their children being in that vulnerable state, which they are in *before* the abuser even arrives on the scene?'

—*Claire, you're way off. Get back on the schools.*

Caroline hesitates. '*All* children are vulnerable,' she says, making parallel lines with her hands, '*all* children are innocent, and *all* of them should be protected.'

'But isn't it true that some children are more vulnerable than others?' Claire asks. 'Isn't that what you've just said? It seems to me' – she pokes the earpiece again – 'that you're asking very tough questions of Rob and the teachers he represents, and asking tough questions of schools and other institutions, but you're not questioning the institution *you* represent, which is the family, which is mothers, and fathers. What role do parents play in a child's abuse?'

BRODERIE ANGLAISE

I was not maid of honour, not even a bridesmaid, but I was dutifully invited, and for this I needed something suitable to wear, something that would signal my grasp of the occasion as well as my transcendence of it; but no matter where I looked – and I spent hours looking – the dress did not exist. No shop possessed it. There is no point explaining now exactly what I had in mind. The details in themselves do not matter, except to say this dress should accommodate my chest without looking matronly or profane; that it should upstage the bridal gown without appearing to do so; and that I was not exactly conscious of these obstinate stipulations, but clicked through the rails of department stores in an agitated dream, like someone brainwashed to accomplish a murder without their consent.

My solution, in the end, was to make the dress myself. At university, I had done quite a lot of sewing. Gemma, one of my housemates, owned a little sewing machine she taught me how to use, though she hardly used it herself. I would run up silly costumes for my friends for Halloween, and basic items for me. 'Run up' was a phrase of my mother's, one I tried not to use, not out loud at least, though it was stuck firmly to the walls of my mind, like the Blu Tack I had used in my rented room, the greasy little coins from which cost me my deposit. But since I had come back to my parents' house the previous summer, the sewing kit had stayed packed away, along with all the items it helped me manufacture. I didn't want to talk about it; I didn't want my mother to know.

Little by little, then, I decided I would make the dress in secret, and pretend it was vintage: my mother's side of the family did not approve of second-hand shopping, and Candice was her niece, her younger sister Amanda's child. My hopeless lunch-break expeditions down the high street became quiet pilgrimages to haberdashery departments, in which I kept my head down, moving quietly among the middle-aged and elderly ladies rattling their knuckles through trays of beads, drawing no more attention than I could help, and asking no questions in case I brought an avalanche of answers down on my head.

Many fabrics presented themselves, and I chose as carefully as I could, avoiding jersey, silk and satin because they would be too difficult to work with, and linen because it would crease. Some bolts of beautiful patterned cotton I put back because I would not be able to make their bold edges join in any logical progression at the seams, or so I told myself, though I think I also quailed at the prospect of them drawing Candice's wedding guests' eyes towards me in the way they had drawn my own.

After a few trips, I had amassed in my bedroom three metres of broderie anglaise, two kinds of thread, a roll of greaseproof paper, a pattern and a roll of calico for practising with, which, along with the sewing kit I dug out from the bottom of the wardrobe, should have been everything I was going to need. Everything, that is, but the sewing machine.

Gemma lived two hundred miles away, and we had not spoken since our final exams. I knew nobody else except my mother who owned a machine. Buying one of my own would have been prohibitively expensive: I was temping as a secretary at the time, work which somehow contrived to pay slightly less than minimum wage, and what I didn't surrender in room and board to my parents was digging me out of an overdraft the bank kept threatening to dissolve. Even if I could have got my hands on my own machine, they were terribly noisy, which left me the same problems I would face if I chose to use my mother's: namely, finding a time when I could sew without detection.

As I mulled this problem over, I was not idle: I did as much as I could behind closed doors, in my bedroom, which had barely changed in my three years away, except that a chest emptied of clothes had been removed to my brother's room. This gave me more space to spread my materials out. I measured myself several times with a floppy fabric tape measure: bust and waist, hips and shoulders. I cut grease-proof panels and tacked them together, then calico panels, and slipped the rig gingerly over my head, warming to the tiny adjustable demands of my ambition, while downstairs my mother cooked dinners from which I excused myself, or watched one of the police dramas she liked so much, and my brother lay lost in the violent immersive dreams of his video games.

Candice and her mother, my Auntie Manda, were often round at our house, ostensibly for the purposes of wedding planning, but also to bask in my mother's envy (the whole marriage business ran on envy, it seemed to me, like a car running on fumes). If I left my door ajar, which I could safely do when there was company downstairs, I could clearly hear them talking above the hiss and snip of the scissors.

'I went to that bakery you told me about,' Candice might say, addressing my mother, who for someone professing not to like cake had been surprisingly full of suggestions, 'and we tried a few samples, didn't we, but the quality just wasn't that good.'

'Much too sweet,' Auntie Manda would agree, sounding faintly offended. 'Really sickly.'

'Well, I thought that might be the case,' my mother would say. 'I've seen some very good things from there, and some not so good, and I thought it might be worth trying, at least, but I thought probably, probably it wouldn't be exactly what you were after.'

'No, it wasn't what we were after,' Auntie Manda would affirm. 'But then we tried the place that Susan suggested, and you liked that one a lot, didn't you, love?'

'I *really* liked that one,' Candice said, drawing out the vowels.

'They did the most beautiful icing,' Auntie Manda said. 'Really beautiful. And the sponge was very moist.'

'Well, that's what you want, isn't it,' my mother said. 'There's nothing worse than dry cake that's too sweet. I'm not a fan of cake, but I know you don't want that.'

'How can you not like cake?' Candice exclaimed. 'These cakes were beautiful. You've got to have a piece at the wedding.'

So it went, the horse-trading of preference and information, with my mother rubbed sore between her sister and her niece until it was time for them to hurry away for another appointment, another opportunity to exhibit their harassment and good fortune, at which point my mother would be able to wash her hands of the whole thing; and although she was reluctant to do this – she wanted, more than anything, I think, to be right at the centre of the wedding – she could at least draw strength from her freedom.

'Lovely to see you,' she would say, trailing them down the hall. 'We'll talk tomorrow. Gosh, you've got so much to do. I don't envy you all that, I really don't. It's a bit like someone else's baby for me. I get to play with her for a while, but then I can give her back!'

They laughed at this – they always laughed – knowing full well that my mother would never have given the baby back if she did not have to. Then their laughter mutated into cries of farewell before the closing door cut them off; and although my mother stood on the near side of this door, her own cries always cut off at exactly the same moment. Then, before she could turn and climb the stairs, I would shut my own door as well. If this seems cruel, I can only say that my mother's weakness in the presence of her sister and her niece filled me not with pity but annoyance – I could not understand why she endured it. What did she think was going to change?

When I could not procrastinate any longer, I gave up the idea of using a machine and began to hand-sew the dress. It was a slow business, very slow indeed. I was not schooled in the art of invisible stitching, only the rough tacks I used to hold the pattern pieces together, and I practised on the calico and then on cuttings from the broderie anglaise before I trusted myself to touch the dress itself. I did this in the hour before and after work, because of the light, and because my mother was generally occupied at those moments, asleep or making dinner. The more time I spent with the fabric, the more enamoured I became of my choice. It was a pale, almost an unnoticeable blue, light as winter sky, the sort of colour that did not declare itself but which would make any off-whites or creams placed beside it look like old dentures in a water glass. The delicate cutwork, scatterings of eyelets lined with satiny buttonhole stitch, receded at distance to no more than a texture, which meant I would not have to worry about the pattern matching up; but closer in it reminded me of bubbles, or birds' prints in snow, and underneath my fingertips it leapt and swirled.

Although I could often avoid Candice when she came round, there was no avoiding the hen party, which took place a week before the wedding. Candice's maid of honour, an old school friend called Katie, had arranged for us to stay the night at a good hotel in town – our own town, that is, not anywhere else. This seemed to me absurd, and I made the mistake of saying so in the early planning stages, threatening to take a cab home at the end of the night, which set Katie and myself at odds with one another for the rest of the affair. Katie, in fact, was the darling of the party, not Candice; she decked Candice out in a polyester veil and tiara, with a plastic penis on a chain around her neck, then steered her through the streets of the city, one bar to the next, using the dazzle of Candice's appearance to reflect attention on to herself. I was reminded of a queen and her adviser: men bantered with Candice as a formality, while Katie sat quietly behind her, waiting to receive her own, more valuable tributes.

At two in the morning, in the hotel bar, I finally spoke to Candice.

'Are you scared?' I asked.

'Of what? Getting married?' Her make-up had slid, her tiara was crooked, and since the shots in Walkabout she had been unable to focus. 'Fuck yeah. But I love him. I love him, you know? And being in love – it's scary.'

Drink had made her honest; for a moment I luxuriated in the false warmth of her confidence, and felt a small flicker of pity, of cousinly love.

'What are you asking her that for?' Katie interrupted.

'It's OK,' Candice said, with a slow wave of her hand.

'No, it's not. She's trying to upset you. What else have you said?'

'Nothing. It was just a question.'

'Well, don't ask her any more questions. You don't want to think about that tonight, do you, babe?'

'She's always asking questions,' Candice said. Her eyes seemed suddenly to close on me, like the fingers of a palsied hand coming together in a grip. 'She's clever.'

'Not that clever,' Katie said, 'if she's asking you something like that.' She took hold of Candice by the wrist and led her away.

When I returned home the following morning, after barely sleeping in the plush hotel, I drew my half-finished dress from the wardrobe drawer where I kept it, wrapped tight in a Debenhams carrier bag, and held it up to the clear summer light. The hem around the bottom rippled. There were tiny puckers in the seams, nothing to which you could point close up, but which gave a slightly lopsided air to the dress's proportions. I immediately tore out all the stitches I had done by hand. There was no way around it: I would have to use my mother's machine.

The machine was a Singer from the 1970s, and it lived in its carrying-case in the cupboard under the stairs. My mother still used it fairly regularly, to make baby clothes for anyone she knew was having a baby, and for occasional repairs, but in years gone by she had made all kinds of things with it, things I still shuddered to imagine myself wearing, but which had at the time seemed like miracles to me: cord dungarees, a little cotton skirt with elastic in the waist. As a child, I had watched in impatient fascination as she heaved the machine on to the kitchen table and proceeded to fiddle with the many knobs and dials that encrusted its beige plastic casing, to open the secret hatch that caught the pins, and to wind and unwind the bobbin at top speed with the treadle. This preparatory stage always took more time than the sewing itself, provided the material didn't bunch up as she passed it beneath the needle, or where the needle was supposed to be, since it moved up and down so fast that it seemed to vanish.

Because my mother had retired early, for reasons she never explained to us, finding time alone with the machine was a challenge. I feigned illness and stayed in bed, abandoning the temporary contract I was under, which meant submitting to endless cups of tea and bowls of soup. The sharp words of my handler at the agency reverberated in my head: despite my education, I had proven myself to be just another one of those unreliable girls. A blackbird sang loudly and variously outside my window. And still my mother did not leave the house.

Many implausible courses of action crossed my mind. I could create some kind of decoy that would draw her away, maybe sending her out for a particular item that could only be located a long drive from home, or arranging for a friend to require her help; I could actually call Gemma (and say what?); I could try a school or college, which would surely have rooms full of such machines going unused over the summer; I could even – impossible in the few days that remained – move out of my parents' house and dedicate a table to sewing in my new flat, or wherever I ended up ... I began to feel as ill as I pretended to be. I welcomed the tea, the soup. My determination not to involve my mother in the process of making the dress, which had been a source of pride in the project's early stages, became the strong light under which my cowardice was fully revealed. While my mother went about her ordinary business downstairs, whatever that might have been, I lay mutinous and unhappy in the chamber of my adolescence, under the same ceiling I had stared at for years, half-making plans that withered and died in the face of her habitual existence.

'How are you feeling this morning?' she would ask, advancing into the sickbed dusk of my room and hovering there, in a light-coloured blouse, like the moon. If I rebuffed her concern, she would turn away, with a pained look on her face, and say, very reasonably, 'Alright, I'll leave you to it. Just call if you need anything.' But if I did not demonstrate quite so clearly my desire to be left alone, she would sink down on the edge of my bed, which tipped the whole mattress towards her, and update me on the wedding. The visits from Candice and Auntie Manda had stopped, now the date was imminent, but she still had plenty to say. 'The flower shop overcharged for the bride's bouquet, did I tell you? They thought she wanted roses, so they charged her for roses, but she didn't, she wanted carnations. Manda says Candice lost six pounds in the last two weeks and they had to get her corset taken in again at the last minute. Uncle David cried at the rehearsal . . .'

Still half-asleep, reclining in the safety of my illness, I let the talk wash over me, and found it mattered less, bothered me less, than it had before, when I had been so determined to counteract it by bringing to the wedding something of which my mother would not know in advance. The head-ache I had invented grew stronger. With only a couple of days to go, I found myself in tears: she was looking after me, in her own, familiar way, and wasn't that all she wanted to do? What, exactly, was wrong with me – why did I hate her for being interested in other people's lives? Wasn't I angry that she wasn't more interested in mine? It was true that when she sat on my bed she rarely asked a question, unless it was about the severity of my pain, or whether I thought I was going to be well enough to attend the service; but that was a kind of anxious sympathy in itself, not to bother me with talking if I'd rather not speak ... There was a strange, sticky quality to these feelings, like a sweet I had found unwrapped in a hidden pocket of my bag, half-melted by its contact with the air and speckled with fluff and dirt. Nevertheless, I put the sweet in my mouth.

'I've been making a dress,' I told her, surprising myself with my confession. 'It's not finished. I don't know if I'll finish it now – I needed to use your sewing machine, and then I got ill.'

She looked at me, astonished. 'You've been making a dress?'

'Yes. To wear to the wedding.'

'Where is it? Can I see it?' She looked around the room, as if it might have been hanging in plain sight all along.

'It's in the wardrobe,' I said, feeling shabby.

'Oh.' She pursed her lips. 'Well, if you feel like showing it to me, I'd like to see it.'

'I would like to show it to you. That's why I brought it up.'

'Shall I get it? Is it hidden? I don't like to rummage through your things.'

'It's in the drawer. In a Debenhams bag.'

Misgivings had already surged through me. As I watched her bend down with some difficulty to open the drawer and retrieve the bag, the headache from which I had genuinely suffered seemed to fade, and a different kind of ache took its place, one much harder to position. She came back to the bed and drew the dress from the bag.

'It's lovely material,' she said. 'Can I draw the curtains?'

Without waiting for an answer, she tore the curtains back from the window, and that same summery light flooded in. I saw the dress clearly in her hands, the fabric she had complimented now diminished in my estimation, limp and blue and childish, like the skirt she had made for me so many years before. But it was too late to stop; soon we were talking through the problems I had experienced with hand-sewing, and the modifications I had made to the pattern I bought, which were designed to nip the dress in firmly at the waist, giving more support.

She insisted we check all my measurements before she would get the sewing machine out. I found myself standing in the middle of my room, my mother's cool hands looping the fabric tape measure around my ribs beneath my pyjamas.

'You haven't allowed that much for the seams,' she said. 'I'd let out another half inch or so. You don't want to do all that sewing then find you can't zip it up.'

'The seams are fine,' I said, not wanting to tell her that I'd done this kind of thing before, that I knew my measurements precisely, though surely my possession of a tape measure and a sewing kit must have stirred her suspicions. If they did, she didn't mention it.

'They seem very slim,' she insisted.

'They're fine.'

'In that case,' she said, pursing her lips again, 'it should be quite simple. Just a straight stitch here and here' – she pointed – 'and zigzag for the rest. Shall I set up the machine? Do you want me to do it? It's just that machine's a bit tricky if you haven't used it before. It can chew things up. I wouldn't want you chewing your lovely material.'

'Is it really that bad?'

'Well, yes,' she said, turning away, 'it's chewed a few things of mine before. But it's your dress – it's really up to you.'

I showered, then, trying to wash the last of the illness away. When I came downstairs the sewing machine was out on the kitchen table, all plugged in and ready to go. I saw my own thread on the bobbin.

'I said I'd do it.'

'I heard the water running,' she said. 'I thought I could save you some time.'

I sat down in front of the shining machine, which was three times the size of Gemma's, and looked so heavy it must have immobilised the table under its weight. There was sweat on my mother's hairline from the effort of setting it up. I couldn't see a manual.

'I'll just show you,' she said, pointing over my shoulder. 'See, this is your straight switch and your zigzag switch. This is your speed – I keep it on six. And this is your reverse, for finishing off. The treadle's quite sensitive so you need a gentle foot.'

Once I ignored all the extra buttons and switches, it wasn't that different from Gemma's. I had a quick practice on some calico ('Gentle foot!'), and then I was ready to try the dress;

23

but the bumpy broderie was a trickier proposition, and almost as soon as I had begun it did exactly what my mother had predicted: some part of the cutwork got caught on the needle, and the fabric was drawn up rapidly into a scrunch.

My mother, who had been pretending to read the paper across the kitchen, instantly reappeared at my side. 'Yes, that's what it tends to do,' she said. 'Broderie can be quite difficult to work with. I was worried about that.' She handed me a little tool for cutting stitches. It took me ten minutes to unpick the ravelled threads. 'Shall we have another try?' she said, when she saw me smooth it out at last. 'I could help. It's no bother. I've finished what I wanted to do.'

'No thank you,' I said. 'I'll do it.'

'I'm just worried that the mistakes are going to start showing soon. I know it's forgiving, the broderie, but probably only up to a certain point. And you've chosen quite a difficult pattern. Do you want me to try?'

I didn't answer. She stood for a moment behind me – I could feel her impatience build – and then she left the kitchen without another word. I sighed heavily: my breath steamed the chrome panel of the Singer's nameplate. The long needle gleamed, poised to descend, and the broderie lay pooled beneath it where I had lined it up to try again. The kitchen was quiet now she had gone, but I didn't move. I was afraid that I was going to ruin the dress, and afraid that I no longer cared – that, no matter how the dress turned out, I had tainted it by breaking the seal on my secret. The clock ticked loudly on the wall above the sink. I heard drawers opening and closing in another room and then I heard my mother's foot-steps returning.

'This is the only other broderie I've got,' she said, in a put-upon voice, as if I had asked her to fetch it. She was out of breath. A garment appeared at my elbow, folded: white broderie anglaise, turning creamy with age. Some kind of old baby's gown. 'You can practise with it, if you want. It doesn't matter. I don't want you ruining your dress.'

'What is it?' I asked. It looked delicate and sentimental.

'Oh, it's nothing. Just your Grandma's christening gown.'

'Really?' I was genuinely surprised; I hadn't even known she possessed such things. 'God, I can't practise on that.'

'Why not?' She shook it out and held it up. Dots of dust swam in the light. It was so small; smaller than any of my own baby clothes, or the baby clothes I'd seen my mother make. 'It's the same kind of material. There's enough.'

'Doesn't it mean something to you? You've kept it this long.'

'No, not really. Not that much.'

I didn't believe her. The gown meant something, even if it wasn't obvious. Her offer was a trick, and either way she'd win: if I practised on the gown, and went through with it all on my own, she could console herself with her sacrifice; and if I couldn't bring myself to ruin the gown, then she could sew my dress herself. She knew I'd done nothing since she left the room. She knew I was frightened to proceed.

'If you don't want it,' I said, trying to come sideways at the problem, 'you could give it to me.' I reached for the gown, but she lifted it away.

'I didn't say I didn't want it. I said you could use it.' Now her tone was curdling from indulgence to irritation; I heard the note of warning, and I ignored it.

'What's the difference?' I asked.

'There is a difference. There's a big difference. This was your Grandma's, and I've had it a long time.'

'Exactly, so why do you want me to spoil it?'

'I don't want you to spoil your dress!'

She was flushed and angry. I looked down at my hands, obscurely angry myself, and ashamed. We stood there in silence for a minute. The prospect of refusing everything she offered, everything, for the rest of our lives, rose in front of me like the ghost of someone I hadn't even known was dead; the vision was far more frightening than the anger I felt. I said, in a sick and cowardly voice, 'I don't have anything of Grandma's. Can I see?'

She passed it to me with only the smallest of hesitations, which seemed to cement my indebtedness to her more than to demonstrate any attachment to the gown on her part. Its broderie was impossibly soft, as if it had been worn and washed and handled a thousand times, though it had probably only been used once, eighty years ago, when the vicar splashed my grandmother's head in the font, and my mother had not even been imagined. I carried it down the hall and up to my bedroom, hearing the sewing machine fire up behind me as she settled to her task. I wondered if she had ever watched my grandmother sew, ever sat spellbound while the needle rose and fell; and I knew that I would never ask.

Lying back down on my sickbed, I examined the gown in more detail. It had little puffed sleeves, pintucks at the waist, and one mother-of-pearl button the size of an apple pip at the nape of the neck. The skirt fell long, far too long, with a starchy stiffness to it, and a hem of lace pointed like a row of incipient fangs.

My mother came upstairs an hour later with the finished dress in her arms. It had looked very small to her, she said, so she'd let the seams out after all.

PATIENCE

Claire arrived at the agency to find Patience already in the waiting area. With her hands folded in her lap and a plastic suitcase on the laminate by her feet, she looked like a travelling salesman or a wartime evacuee, someone thrown on the mercy of others. The receptionist stamped the paperwork and said, 'She's all yours.'

Patience stood up.

'Am I meant to shake your hand,' Claire said, 'or is that not the right thing? Have you been here long? I couldn't get away from work, and then the roundabout was closed.'

'Do not worry,' Patience replied, with a sweet and stupid expression on her face, 'I have been happy sitting here, watching the world go by,' even though the view through the agency's front windows was of a deserted self-storage facility.

Claire steered Patience out to the car and settled her in the passenger seat, with the suitcase on her lap. Patience made no comment about the car's cloudy paintwork; she said nothing as it clunked into gear or rounded corners too fast, and Claire wondered grimly how her mother would respond to an unflusterable presence like this.

'Tell me about your mother,' Patience said, as if she could hear what Claire was thinking. It was a sensible guess, a simple question, but Claire was momentarily silenced by it.

'I did that enormous interview,' she said. 'I filled in that enormous questionnaire. She's still what she is.'

'So she is still difficult. Can you tell me about a difficulty she has presented in the last few days?'

There must have been a dozen examples, but the words 'difficult' and 'difficulty' – though Claire might have used them herself in the interview; Patience might simply be following her lead – got in the way. They presented Claire's mother as a kind of obstruction, like a tree toppled across the road. They implied that Claire had imagined her that way too.

'Let's call her *independent*. Or *eccentric*. All right?'

'I have offended you.'

'No, no, you haven't, not at all. I just want us to think about the words we're using. Older women are dehumanised enough already, don't you think?'

Every weekday, first thing in the morning, Claire visits her mother. She strips her and washes her with perineal wipes, going carefully around the twisted pink tubes of her haemorrhoids. She helps her into clean Depends, gets her dressed and breakfasted, and settles her in the gold brocade chair by the window. Then she goes to work: she works at the university library, as a subject librarian for the English department. At the end of the day, she goes back to her mother again and makes dinner. Often she stays until her mother is in bed, then drives back to her own flat, where half her books are still in boxes, and sleeps a sleep that clenches her jaw. The flats of her molars feel strange to her these days, unfamiliar formations too close to the ground.

She spends the weekends with her mother too, except for Sunday afternoons, when she insists on disappearing for a few hours. Her mother complains only moderately about this. Claire might look in the shops, or see a film, or – more recently – go for a slow swim in the adults-only lane at the leisure centre, which leaves her hungry and hollow for the rest of the day, and makes her mother moan about the chlorine smell.

It has been this way, or getting this way, for a long time now, at least twelve years; though when she thinks back, it is hard to recall her mother not needing attention. There are few dividing moments in the smooth run of years, few abrupt accelerations. The first angina attack, perhaps. The arthritis diagnosis. The biggest marker, really, was left by Claire's brother, Ross – his moving away. He lives in Hong Kong now, doing something high-stakes, financial. She pictures him working in a skyscraper mirrored like a pair of expensive sunglasses.

'Who's that in the car?' Claire's mother wants to know. She has watched them park from the living room window, from her chair.

'That's my friend Patience.'

'Patience? What sort of a name is that? Who makes new friends in their forties?'

'I've brought her to see you.'

'You've left her outside.'

Her mother's eyes are pink again. Conjunctivitis. They can't seem to get rid of it: she rubs them, she wipes it everywhere, then she catches it again.

'Bring her in then, if she's come to see me. I never get any visitors. Or do I have to pass the test first? Are you going to check the bathroom's not a mess?'

'Mum. I'm going away for a while.'

'You know I can't manage the bathroom. I've been waiting for you. Where is the shopping? Is it in the car?'

'Mum, listen.'

'All right, all right. You're going away. Where are you going?' Her mother's nails are dirty. It is difficult for her to wash her hands properly: arthritis has turned each finger to a bubbled question mark.

'To the Netherlands. To Holland.'

'Oh, *Holland*. I knew a Dutchman once. He was really short. They're supposed to be tall, the Dutch, but this one was really, really short. He was completely fixated on me, even though I was far too tall for him. We would've looked ridiculous together.'

'I'm going to Haarlem,' Claire says. 'They've given me a fellowship there.'

The jammy eyes blink. 'I'm sorry, I don't know what that is.'

★

Patience brings her case inside, and Claire carries the shopping to the kitchen. As she unpacks, she can hear the charged silence of her mother sizing Patience up.

'What's *your* story? Or do I want to know?'

'Do you like stories?' Patience replies.

Claire's mother snorts. 'It's an expression. You've never heard that expression before? It means, who are you, why are you here?'

'Yes, Jacqueline, I've heard it before.'

Putting plums in the bowl, Claire flinches. Her mother calls out, 'You hear that? She thinks we're on first-name terms already. No Ms Pettifer for you, is there?'

'I'm sorry. Is that how you'd prefer to be addressed?'

'I'd prefer that you asked me first. Is that all right?'

'Yes. And you may call me Patience.'

'Oh, may I? *May* I? Claire!'

Her mother is leaning forward hawkishly in the wing chair. Patience stands with her hands by her sides.

'I don't want her. Take her away.'

'I'm not taking her away.'

'You think I don't know what she is? I know what she is. She's rude. She's got no social sense. Have you heard how she's speaking to me?'

'Mum—'

'It's not a good start. At the very least they ought to be able to make a good start.'

'If I may,' Patience says. 'Ms Pettifer, I apologise. I should have asked how you would like to be addressed.'

'That's a very basic thing, I would have thought. It's very basic to ask a person how they want to be spoken to.'

'You are right, of course. I should have been more respectful. I will remember this in future.'

'All right, all right. Don't creep. What time is it? Did you bring any of those biscuits?'

Claire's mother is surprisingly greedy, given how thin she's become. A greedy little bird. She pecks and pecks at biscuits all day. She likes her glass of sweet Chardonnay at night. Claire sends Patience through with the biscuits, a small offering, a treat, to cement the bond.

'You're still here,' her mother says when Claire emerges. There are crumbs in the hollows of her chest. 'When're you off? You shouldn't keep all those little Dutchmen waiting. Watch out for them, though. They're naughty. They're very naughty on the Continent.'

'I'll call you when I land.'

'We're all the same size lying down!'

When Claire has gone off in her cheap little car – though not without sitting behind the wheel for five minutes, in full view of the neighbours, like a sack of potatoes – Jacqueline turns to Patience and examines her pale hair, her light, smooth skin like a twenty-year-old's. Patience, in turn, seems to be examining Jacqueline. No surprise there: Jacqueline has always been a striking woman. People feel compelled to look. Why shouldn't Patience feel compelled too?

'You could call me *sensei*,' Jacqueline says, inspired. 'Do you know what that means? It means teacher.'

'It also means *person born before another*, did you know that?'

'I was born before you, wasn't I?'

'Technically,' Patience says, 'I was not born.'

'Oh, so what. So you were put together from a kit. You weren't and then you were – that's being born. Do you know where *I* was born?'

'In Crystal Palace.'

'Wrong! That's where I lived. Did Claire tell you that? I *lived* in Crystal Palace; I was *born* in Shirley Oaks. My grandfather was one of the firemen who put out the Crystal Palace fire. The great fire, when it all burned down. He was only young then, and really handsome, my grandfather. My father was, too. Really, really handsome men. My grandfather went in and rescued one of the office ladies. She'd inhaled a lot of smoke, but she lived. She was grateful to him all her life. I think she loved him. He lost all the hair off his right arm bringing her out, but it grew back much thicker than before. Like a kiwi fruit.'

'That is extraordinary.'

'Is it? He was just my Grandpa to me. Imagine if he'd married that woman! She was a nightmare. Completely hopeless. She used to send him a card on his birthday, a card at Christmas, even after my father was born. *Henry, I remember you always*. He wasn't a fireman then. He went into finance. He got absolutely filthy stinking rich. You wouldn't believe the way my father was raised. He had butter every day, even when there was rationing. If you've got money, you can get whatever you like. It's all gone now, obviously.'

'May I ask what happened?'

'What do you think? What always happens. Crooks.'

Patience cooks dinner, fishcakes and broccoli, all acceptable, but then the fishcakes are already made up. Afterwards it's time for the one soap that Jacqueline can bear. Claire never watches it with her – she says it rots her brain, as if she'd never watched all those stupid teen programmes when she was still at home! – but Patience does.

'I can't imagine what you'll get from it,' Jacqueline says. 'I need a bit of drama, stuck in here all day. What use is it to you?'

'I am interested in what interests you.'

'Suit yourself. I can't stand this woman—' she points at the screen '—this woman here, Christina. Her husband's having an affair and she doesn't even know. It's so obvious!'

Jacqueline accepts her glass of wine in time for the news. It makes the headlines bearable. 'Look at the state of it,' she says. 'Nothing but crooks, the lot of them, murderers and crooks, and nobody staying where they ought to be, just buggering up their own countries then coming over here.'

'Migration has certainly increased in the last five years,' Patience says, 'but did you know that emigration from the UK to other countries has grown three hundred per cent?'

'There's something wrong with you, I think, if you can't make a life for yourself in your own country.'

'But Jacqueline, your son has emigrated to Hong Kong.'

'They needed him. He was offered a job. He didn't just turn up on the doorstep without a penny to his name.'

'I think you are confusing immigrants with refugees. Immigrants make a rational choice to leave their home countries. Refugees are driven out by conflict or persecution, in fear of their lives.'

'Call it what you like, it's all about money at the end of the day.'

'Extreme poverty may be a factor.'

'Poverty! Like there's not any poverty here. Aren't I living in poverty? All I own's this house, and what use is that to me?'

Claire would have lost her temper by now. She would have got up on her high horse about how her mother's home ownership meant that she wasn't allowed to voice her opinions any more. Never mind that Claire had bought a flat and still forced *her* opinions down everybody's throats. Apparently, if you're talking against your own, it's allowed. She once stormed out of the house and didn't come back for two days. But Patience just watches the news, or pretends to.

'What will you do?' Jacqueline asks when it's time for bed. 'Will you sleep?'

'In a manner of speaking.'

Patience offers to help Jacqueline up the stairs, as if Jacqueline is a cripple, as if she can't manage her own house.

'You must be joking. Do you joke?'

'I joke.'

'Let's crack it out, then, shall we? Sooner rather than later.'

Jacqueline lies down, but the smoke alarm's little green eye in the darkness, and the thought of Patience doing God knows what downstairs, keep her alert. Where's Claire got to? Jacqueline would not be surprised to discover that she'd wanted a break from her mother, made up this fellowship, whatever *that* is, elaborated it somehow, so as to give herself a nice holiday somewhere, or maybe even just a holiday at home, five miles away, safe in the knowledge that she wouldn't run into her mother, since Jacqueline hardly ever leaves the house. Maybe there's a man. Could there be a man? There hasn't been for years.

She gets her reading glasses and the *Tatler* back into her lap. Then she hears a noise outside. A step.

'You can stop slinking around.'

'Is there anything I can do for you?' Patience looks exactly the same: no nightclothes for her, no taking off of the face. 'You can't sleep.'

'I never sleep. I haven't slept for years.'

'That must be terrible for you.'

'Must it? I'm used to it. Wee Willie Winkie, that's me. Up and down with my candlestick. But you know what *that's* like, don't you?'

'Your experience will be different to mine, Ms Pettifer.'

'Oh for God's sake, I'm in my knickers here. Call me Jacqui.'

'Are you in pain?'

'When am I not?'

'Would you like a sedative? A camomile tea? Maybe a whisky?'

'My daughter wouldn't approve of you giving me whisky.'

'Jacqui, I don't think she would mind at all. She wants me to make you comfortable.'

'Comfortable! What a horrible word. Like a big fat person lying on a load of pillows. You know I used to have a 24-inch waist? My husband could put his hands right round me. Don't hover, come in if you're coming in. He was a bastard, Claire's father, with great big wonderful hands ...'

Haarlem is higgledy-piggledy, like a child's idea of a town, the buildings flame-coloured and edged with what looks like icing. Claire is given an office in the arts tower, a library card, the use of a bicycle she is too afraid to ride, and a mid-term let with high ceilings and unwashed windows. There are welcome drinks at the Fellows' Institute. Claire sips a glass of warm white wine, her first in twelve years. All the Haarlemers speak flawless English with American accents, but when Claire turns away they drop back into Dutch. She meets, briefly, the director of the library, a horse-faced woman with a flaking scalp, and the term's other fellows – a lady from Shanghai who wears business attire, a large American in a Los Lobos T-shirt, and a compact, curly-haired professor from London, quite handsome, who stops talking to her as soon as he grasps that she's not an academic.

She has proposed to study an initiative being run by the Haarlem university library in which 'seniors' are invited to participate in archival work. They are bussed in from the suburbs, a special arrangement with a local retirement home; they work, they have lunch in the library canteen, and then they're taken home again. The social inclusion of this appeals to her, the valuing of Haarlem's elderly population, their special relationship to the past. She envisages using her study to recommend something similar at home. But when she begins to interview the librarians, she finds them unenthusiastic: they tell her that the seniors work too slowly to be of any use.

'They just talk to each other,' says Annika, a woman Claire's age with a permanent ironic expression, 'all the time talking, and nothing gets finished. I wouldn't mind if they were making progress, but they have to leave things and come back to them a week later, and they never remember what they were doing. Then they won't ask. They just do it how they like, and when we find the mistakes – *if* we find the mistakes – we have to fix them all ourselves. Hugo there—' she points to a gentleman with alarmingly long ears, '—wrote the catalogue numbers on a set of original documents *in pen.*'

'So it isn't a rewarding process?'

'Rewarding for whom?'

The seniors, then, must be getting something from it. Claire speaks with Sanne, a soft, sloping woman whose fleshy upper arms never move, as if she is alive still only from the elbows, only in her hands. Sanne sits at the archiving desk with her friend Emma and rummages through the old papers they've been given to assess, internal documents, some of which need to be shredded.

'Oh, yes, I like coming here,' Sanne says. 'I like to see the young people. I like to feel useful.'

'Oh yes,' says Emma, 'it is nice to feel useful again.'

'The only problem I would say is that they do not have real butter in the sandwiches in the canteen, and that I am only allowed one cup of coffee.'

'You're right, it's not real butter.'

'I asked her, Annika, if I could have another cup – I was tired, you see – and she said oh, no, you can't have more coffee, we've budgeted for one coffee each, and if I give you an extra coffee then everybody is going to want one.'

'Yes, she did say that.'

'I said I would drink it in secret, nobody would know, but she wouldn't agree. I don't understand. It's not even proper coffee; it's just instant coffee. What's the big deal?'

'You're right, it's only instant.'

'I think she could give it to me if she wanted to. She just likes holding it over us. I don't think she has anyone at home. No wedding ring, you see.'

'*Geen kinderen*,' Emma agrees.

When Claire finishes in the library for the day and steps out into the warm evening, she is overwhelmed with a sense of desolation. The Haarlemers are all hurrying somewhere, by bike or on foot, but there is nowhere for Claire to go, nobody for her to see. Into this emptiness rushes a vision of her mother, hundreds of miles away, alone with a robot. She walks around the park and rings home.

'Claire, I can't talk right now, Patience has made a chicken Kiev.'

'But are you all right?'

'*Well* – if you mean, are my hands still on fire? then the answer's yes, but that's not going to change, is it?'

'Can you put Patience on?'

'No, not really, she's doing the dishes. Bye!'

Claire circles the park, avoiding the pubs, the quiet apartment. She thinks of her brother, Ross, the traveller, the now-expatriate, who would surely be completely at ease in a European city at night, would know where to go and what to say, how to focus on the world around him.

The park is planted with tulips – of course – great stiff hordes of them, their stems completely rigid, their petals sloping in sharply at the tips. Claire is like that somehow: tulip-shaped. The opening of her, the interface, is tiny, tiny, the interior surprisingly large. And her mother is somehow the opposite. She is all surface area, everything shamelessly on show.

Patience is a good listener; and, it turns out, a wonderful baker. Jacqueline looks forward to a warm fruit scone at four o'clock. Then she begins to expect it. When Jacqueline's in bed, Patience waits downstairs, open-eyed, all night, like a Roman soldier. And she is tireless about the housework, full of respect for Jacqueline's things. 'This is very fine tweed, Jacqui. It must be cleaned very carefully.' 'This dish mustn't go in the dishwasher. The pattern will fade.'

'I wish you'd stop pretending to care so much,' Jacqueline says to her one day.

'May I ask why?'

'Because it's a load of rubbish. You didn't choose to be here, did you?'

'No. But were I able to make a choice, I would choose to stay with you. You are a fascinating woman.'

'Oh, I'm fascinating, am I?'

'Why do you sound surprised?'

'I'm not surprised. I suppose you're programmed with things like that to say, aren't you? I suppose your memory banks are all prepared.'

'I am made to appreciate what is most unique and interesting about the person I live with. It's a very complex process, and my response to you is unique, because you are a unique person, and our conversations follow a unique pattern. However, it might satisfy you to know that although every person is unique, some are more unique than others, if I may use such a tautology; and you are certainly among a small minority of the population, both in terms of your life experiences and your psychological profile. That is why I question your scepticism. You can be sceptical of me, of course, but you cannot be sceptical of what I'm saying. I think you know this about yourself.'

'I don't know what I know about myself,' Jacqueline says. 'My children used to find me interesting when they were children. But then they got older, and they stopped. So I stopped thinking of myself that way. You try believing you're worth a damn when every time you open your mouth they roll their eyes at you. They'd come home from school and bolt straight upstairs. I made them sit and eat their dinner with me, but they couldn't wait to leave the table.'

'I am very sorry to hear that. But, you know, this is very common behaviour for adolescents. You must not think it had anything to do with you.'

'Is it common behaviour to abandon your elderly mother to a *machine*?'

'Actually,' says Patience, 'it is.'

Although the university library is open at the weekend, Annika is not there, and neither are the seniors, which leaves Claire with little to do between Friday at five and Monday at nine. She takes a cruiser rather dutifully up the Spaarne, past narrow houses with tiled roofs, and an enormous brown windmill that looks like it has been constructed by giants out of plywood and Cook's matches. She disembarks and walks around Park Schoteroog, looking at the pleasure boats out on the lake. There are none of the flax fields Mary Shelley noted in her letters, no bundles of river-soaked flax drying against the trees. Maybe that's for the best: she'd complained about the stink.

Claire is passionately interested in Mary Shelley. It is not an informed passion, not exactly; there is something serendip-itous and irrational in it. When she was sixteen, she bought Shelley's second novel, *Mathilda*, from a cheap bookstall, and read it in a sort of daze, not understanding much of the prose, but feeling troubled by its effects. The long lost father, his incestuous love for his child, had a strange appeal; and certain phrases and passages lodged themselves in her memory and seemed to shine, like the notion that Happiness, not God, 'sits enthroned above the clouds', or Mathilda's speech about prisons: 'A little patience, and all will be over; aye, a very little patience; for, look, there is the key of our prison; we hold it in our own hands, and are we more debased than slaves to

44

cast it away and give ourselves up to voluntary bondage?' It had taken her a few more years to understand that the key Mathilda was talking about was the power to kill oneself.

As part of her fellowship, Claire will be required to run an informative session for the library staff, something that will enable them to learn from the professional practice of colleagues overseas. This prospect gradually fills her mind as she walks beside the lake. She has prepared nothing, and though the session is not scheduled until late in her stay, she already feels anxious. The Haarlem library is extremely well organised. The librarians, like Annika, seem competent and ambitious, already familiar with current best practice, probably more familiar than Claire herself. They all seem to have Information Studies degrees, whereas Claire ascended to her position through sheer endurance, beginning at the bottom, as a shelving assistant, and getting to know her library inside out, its cold basements and miles of clanging shelves, every miserable faux-Egyptian lintel, every bubbling radiator. She developed a protective, proprietary sense of custodianship as she watched the people come and go and the building endure. Still, it took years before she distinguished herself enough to be promoted to full librarian, and years more to become what she is now. She has proven herself to be capable and reliable, outlasting the young men and women with Librarianship MAs and no common sense (one of them failed a shelving test!) who were appointed above her.

Now she is known, at work, for possessing all the answers, but they are answers that do not travel: where to look for missing periodicals, how to game the system to stretch your budget, which professors will explode if you're tardy with their reference lists. It's a role she has self-constructed from whatever came to hand, like one of those birds who build their nests out of shreds of old carrier bag. She knows the higher-ups think she isn't dynamic enough: they'd like someone more dazzling, better published, in her role, someone they can put on the marketing materials to make the prospective students go, Wow, their librarians look like *that*? They don't want her moony, ruddy face, her frizzy hair, her unpainted nails in the open-toed sandals. So she's made herself indispensable instead. When they look at her, the managers, she wants them to see a stalwart, one who cannot be dislodged without imperilling the whole operation.

What of this could possibly translate to a conventional training session? She cannot say what she really thinks – that the arcane, the Byzantine, the unrepeatable, are the true essence of a library – not in a climate of rabid standardisation and frictionless transferrals of knowledge. It would seem like a daft romance. All the Haarlemers, with their shiny qualifications, would grow impatient, shift in their chairs, question her right to speak. She pictures the director of the library folding her arms tight at the back of the room, and knows what she needs to do. The work with the seniors is sluggish, anyway; she can put it aside for a few days, and turn her attention to recent Information Studies journals. She will find something current to talk about.

Jacqueline loves to watch the finches at the feeder outside, so bright, so quick, so glamorous, with their sturdy little beaks.

They put her in a sort of dream. But the dream won't come today. She is distracted. To Patience, who is cleaning – she has pulled the fridge right away from the wall – Jacqueline says, 'What did you mean, then? About my psychological profile being so unique?'

'The most striking feature is your narcissism. My assessment puts you at an average of zero point eight two on the Narcissism Spectrum Scale.'

Jacqueline feels adrenalised, suddenly thrilled. 'What a load of rubbish,' she says. 'I've never heard such rubbish in my life.'

'One notable feature of your condition is that it renders you unable to believe that you have a condition at all. Narcissists can never admit that they are narcissists because they can never admit to being at fault.'

'I've got faults. I admit to faults all the time.'

'I appreciate it seems that way to you.'

'It doesn't *seem* that way. That's the way it is.'

'Would you like me to respond, or would you prefer to leave it there? I can see you are upset.'

'Oh no, by all means. Why stop now?'

'I recognise the sarcasm in your tone, but nonetheless I think you are pleased to discuss yourself. I will proceed until you tell me to stop.

'It is true that sometimes you admit to small indiscretions that can in some sense be described as faults. However, you tend to present them as mistakes that anyone could have made, and which are not to be held against you. You have a very interesting defence that underpins most of your day-to-day statements, which is – to put it simply – *I am doing my best.*'

'I am!'

Patience nods. 'Yes, you really believe this. You believe you are doing your best in all things, and that therefore any faults or errors cannot be considered faults or errors as such, because they have arisen from the best intentions. This is what you might think of as the 'human' defence. It says, in all sincerity, *I am only human* – as if being human were proof against error, rather than a guarantee that errors will be made.'

'Hilarious,' Jacqueline says. 'That's hilarious coming from you. I can't believe I've got a robot lecturing me on how I think I'm incapable of making mistakes.'

'Are you implying that I also believe myself to be incapable of making mistakes?'

'Well? Don't you?'

'It is not a belief.'

One day, walking further north through the city, Claire discovers a deconsecrated church that contains a small psychiatry museum. Inside are phrenological sculptures that break the brain into jigsaw pieces, and Rorschach blots that look to her like nothing at all. In the main exhibition hall stands a brown leather day bed, a sort of proto-recliner that doesn't straighten up, with straps all the way down both sides, wrist straps and ankle straps and even a strap for the chest. It is nearly two hundred years old, and reminds Claire immediately of the gold brocade chair at her mother's, which reclines if you pull a switch. The plaque calls it a 'compulsory chair', and explains that it was used to treat mental illness in the 1850s. Doctors had thought people's brains were inflamed, and that if they kept them immobilised the swelling would go down, but instead the patients developed haemorrhoids and bedsores and arthritis, and went even crazier because they couldn't move around. It actually says that: 'crazier'.

Next to the plaque is a poster:

LIVING MUSEUM
Could you sit in the compulsory chair for an hour?
Come and help us bring our exhibits to life!

Claire approves, instantly, of this project – she likes it when the public gets involved – and it comes naturally to her to volunteer, almost as a civic duty, even though this isn't her town, her country, even. And isn't that what people said you should do if you were lonely? Volunteer for something? She goes to the desk and puts her name down, and they tell her they will text her to set a performance time. She leaves with a hope, a prospective lightness, she's grateful for.

Back in her office, someone knocks. It is the American with the Los Lobos T-shirt – though today he wears the Grateful Dead – who also has an office in the tower. His name is Jerome and he's an art historian, visiting from a university she's never even heard of.

'Hallabassee County College for the Arts. It's basically a money-laundering operation for white-collar criminals.

They send us their filthy kids with their filthy tuition and we wash 'em all clean with four years of keg parties and classes on *Breaking Bad*. Really, it's a disaster.'

He says this standing in her doorway, as tall and wide as the frame, his eyes scanning every inch of the room.

'Oh, you've got a great view. You've got the Spaarne. Have you been on the water yet? Have you been to Mooie Nel? So peaceful. Seriously, though, Hallabassee, it's a graveyard. I've been there six years and I'm never getting out, not unless I win some huge grant or someone decides to make a movie about Pieter Claesz and pay me for consulting.'

'Is that likely to happen?'

'Pieter Claesz? Are you crazy? My guy did nothing but paint still lifes. He had a son. Guess what the son did? He painted still lifes too. It'd be the world's most boring cinematic experience. Pieter Claesz arranges crabs and shrimp for half an hour. Pieter Claesz paints a glass of wine but never drinks it. Fuck, you'd kill yourself. Are you hungry? Are you heading out? I found this great place for *bitterballen*. Have you tried *bitterballen* yet?'

Bitterballen are deep-fried and horrifyingly delicious. Claire eats more than she'd usually eat, because nothing seems excessive in the presence of this man, who puts away four times as much as her, and three Amstels. She has an Amstel too. It shoots straight to her thighs and makes them buzz.

'So how do you find the Dutch?' asks Jerome. 'The *Nederlanders*? Do you find them odd? I remember the first time I came here, when I was a postgrad. I couldn't believe it. I mean, I'd heard how rude they were – my supervisor, he warned me – but you can't believe it till you hear it.'

'I wouldn't call them rude.'

'Oh really? But you know what I mean, right? You need to lose some weight: that's what they said to me. They took me for a bike ride, and it was a hot day, and I was sweating, because you sweat, right? And they were all healthy and fucking *athletic*, and they laughed at me and said, Jerome, you need to lose some weight, you're going to die!' He slaps his gut. 'Obviously I didn't pay any attention.'

'I like them, though. I think if they were rude I wouldn't like them. Maybe I'd say they were more ... direct?'

'See, to me, that's a really *indirect* way of saying someone's rude. It's a very *English* way.' He pauses. 'I bet you think I'm a total jingoist now, don't you? I bet you think I go around typing everyone by nationality. I don't. I just think there's some truth to it, there's got to be some truth, to the national character. It interests me. How could it not? I'm big and loud and greedy and I talk too much. I'm such an American.' He wipes his mouth. 'Have you tried *Stroopwafel* yet? I know a great place.'

Jerome arrived in Haarlem at the same time as Claire, but already he has taken possession of the city, establishing a routine that makes him mysteriously unavailable in the mornings, emerging from his flat only for lunch, after which he visits the Franz Hals Museum, 'To check in with my guy', before settling down in his office. He works until at least ten or eleven at night, only venturing out for snacks, or to hover in his colleagues' doorways and talk about whatever's on his mind. Claire gets used to this rather quickly. She looks forward to his visits; sometimes she goes out with him to eat. He always knows somewhere worth trying.

Narcissist! The word swirls in Jacqueline's mind; she turns back to the finches, but she's more distracted than ever. Does Patience think she's a person now? Does she think she knows something about how real people work? What even is a narcissist, exactly? She gets the Collins dictionary out of the cupboard, and as she reads the definitions she has to laugh.

'What's funny?' Patience asks.

'Oh, nothing. I just looked up your word "narcissist", that's all. I thought I'd see what it really meant.'

'Would you like me to define it for you?'

Jacqueline reads aloud: '*Narcissism: An exceptional interest in or admiration for oneself, especially one's physical appearance.* Vanity, we used to call it, but I suppose that sounds too Biblical for you.'

'Vanity can be one part of it, of course.'

'What is it? Is it because I care about my appearance? I'll have you know that's actually a very sociable thing to do. It's sociable to make an effort, that's what my mother told me. It's other people who have to look at you all day.'

'It is not about your appearance.'

'Just because I'm stuck at home now, just because I never see anyone apart from you, I'm supposed to stop straightening my hair? Should I stop bathing too?'

'This is a very old dictionary you are consulting. The term also has clinical meanings.'

'Oh, I'm not finished yet. This is a good one. *Sexual satisfaction derived from contemplation of one's own physical or mental endowments*! —You know, at this point I'd take it, I really would.'

'Jacqui, are you sexually dissatisfied?'

'Oh for God's sake.'

'You are entitled to a sexual existence, whatever your age.'

'What do you know about sex? You haven't even got any bits, have you? You're all smooth down there like a doll. Not even that – it looks like you're wearing trousers, but they're just part of you, aren't they? You've got no underneath.'

The day of the training session arrives. Claire has spent far more time preparing her materials than she meant to, mainly because the topic she chose – standardisation of library layout – has been discussed more than she'd anticipated, despite its essential tediousness. The session is basically a literature review, though she has built in a small group exercise, in which she challenges the staff to create and rationalise a sensible layout for a new library. She has created and laminated four sets of a library floor space with moveable blocks of shelving for this purpose, something which took her a full day to accomplish. It's an effort she thought they would appreciate, but she spots two of the younger participants rolling their eyes at one another when she hands the sets out, and feels herself flush.

The session passes in a blur, with minimal participation. No one seems engaged, and Claire cannot blame them. This is how she's felt at most of the mandatory training she's suffered – superior, detached. There are two minutes for questions at the end, and the usual recalcitrant silence ensues. It's a good sign, she tells herself, in a way. It means she's told them everything they needed to know.

Eventually, a hand goes up.

'Yes, Annika?'

'This is more of a comment than a question,' Annika says, 'but I feel very uncomfortable with this homogenising process that's going on in librarianship, like we're trying to turn everything into McDonald's, everything being done in exactly the same way all over the world, when before we had all these independent restaurants that served different kinds of foods from different traditions, and were just more representative of what actually the human experience of discovering and taking in knowledge really is, something personal and unrepeatable, not this corporate bullshit, pardon my language.'

Scattered laughter.

'I mean, it's my profession, it's how things work, and of course I have to do it, but I can still feel – you know, in myself – *resistant* to this process, *critical* about it.'

'Yes, Annika,' says the director from the back of the room, 'we are all familiar with your opinions on this subject' – but there's a warmth in her tone that Claire finds utterly bewildering. Something throbs behind her eyes. She feels a heat in her throat, the sting that augurs tears, and she blunders the session to a close. The director vanishes. Everyone else filters out, except for Annika, who says, 'I upset you.'

'Oh, no, you didn't.' Claire goes from table to table, collecting the laminated sets. 'I'm fine.'

'Well, that's good.' Annika pauses. 'I'm going to go meet a couple of friends for a drink. Do you want to come?'

Claire would certainly like a drink, but the thought of sitting there with Annika, accepting Annika's pity, knowing that she thinks Claire is some sort of repulsive globalising capitalist of knowledge, is awful.

'Thank you, but I've already got plans.'

This isn't entirely a lie. Tonight she is meeting Jerome at the Franz Hals – he's made friends with the security guard, who lets him stay late – so that he can show her the painting of Claesz's he is working on. But there are two hours to kill before that.

Jacqueline's sleep deteriorates. It's the rich food Patience is making; the pain she cannot cure. At night she lies awake looking at the smoke alarm, but she doesn't put the lamp on, she doesn't bother to read, and Patience never comes.

In the daytime, she channel-surfs. She remembers how she once hid the flicker and told Claire it had disappeared. It hadn't: she was sitting on it – the buttons nudged her piles – but Claire didn't think to check beneath her mother's bony bum, and she spent all night hunting, pulling up the cushions, putting them back. When Jacqueline had finally stood up to go to bed, and the flicker fell to the floor, Claire froze, then burst into tears. Her mother's protestations of innocence made no difference to her. She flounced from the house, and did not return until the following night.

There is no point hiding the flicker with Patience, though. Patience can probably change the channels with her mind.

One day, presented with the reliable fruit scone, Jacqueline snaps, 'I've filled my boots with those things.'

'You don't like the recipe?'

'It's not the recipe, it's the *sameness*. Same shape, same texture, same seven bloody sultanas in every one. Do you count them or what?'

'I'll put it away for later.'

'Feed it to the birds. I told you, I've lost my taste.'

And what does Patience do? She feeds it to the birds! Jacqueline has to watch her out there in the little back garden, poking broken scones into the bird-feeder, scattering the rest of them on the ground: so much food that the finches can't contain themselves but come fluttering in and dart around Patience's feet. Or is it that Patience's feet aren't feet to them, don't register as living things, but as the base of the folded washing line, or tyres on a car in the road?

Claire would not have fed the scones to the birds. She would have known to put them away for later.

Pieter Claesz's *Covered Table with Pie* depicts an elaborate cornucopia of fruits, nuts, olives, sliced bread and sliced lemons, a cut-open pie, and a large basket overflowing with grapes. The grapes and the olives and the goblet of white wine gleam wetly like the surface of an eye.

'Isn't it incredible?' Jerome says. 'There's so much written about this painting already. I don't know what I was thinking.

Like, I've been reading Arthur Goldberg again. Have you ever read any Goldberg? His criticism is outstanding. The things he can make a painting do!'

'See, to me, that's the wrong way around.'

'Oh,' Jerome says, 'you're a *Romantic*. You gotta get over that.'

They walk through the empty galleries, past rows of imposing oils, and he talks about the importance of mastering one's texts – he often calls paintings 'texts'. He begins to tell her about a PhD student he supervises, 'this poor girl', who hasn't realised what a scam Hallabassee is, who works so many part-time service jobs to pay her tuition fees that she can't get a grip on Claesz; and then he tells her about another student he is meant to supervise next year, a young man, barely twenty-two, who is determined to write about anatomical aberrations in 'Andrea del Sarto' and Rob Liefeld's *Captain America*. When Claire pulls a face at this, Jerome says, 'I know, right? Who's interested in *Browning*?'

They sit on a bench in a hall full of Hals, groups of men in cavalier costumes gathered around banqueting tables, making merry, all their heads at different angles, as if they're each inclining to a different voice.

'I nearly did a PhD,' she says.

'Oh yeah?' Grease shines on Jerome's upper lip.

'I wanted to write about Mary Shelley. Not *Frankenstein*, a different book. *Mathilda*. You won't have read it. Nobody's ever heard of it. It wasn't published in her lifetime. She sent it home to England, and it just disappeared. It turned up later, in the 1950s.'

'What was your thesis?'

'My *thesis*, God.' She remembers the potential supervisor she'd approached, his stained teeth as he'd asked the same question. 'Well – I was twenty-three. Everything was so dramatic. Everybody in that book, except Woodville – he's the love interest, kind of – everybody is living a very trau-matised life, and there was a lot of stuff about trauma going on at the time, so I thought, OK, I'll do that.'

'Right, but what was your *thesis*?'

'I'm getting to that,' she says, 'if you'll let me talk. *Mathilda* isn't – it's not what you'd call a masterpiece. It's quite an indulgent book. It doesn't have that central sort of *spine* that the monster and the experiments give to *Frankenstein*, so all the hand-wringing and the hysterics and the long speeches start to feel a bit baggy and ridiculous, but at the same time somehow purer. It fails, but it fails in this sort of *pure* way. I wanted to write about that – about how the book's trying to impress the extremity of its trauma on the reader, and just ignoring everything else a novel's meant to do.' She feels herself reddening again. 'Stylistics of Trauma, or something, I called it.'

'I guess it's a smart play,' Jerome says. 'Going for the minor works.'

This is what people tend to think – that Claire's project was cynical, calculated – and usually she's happy to let them think it, because it's less shameful than admitting she loves the book, finds Mathilda's predicament moving, and wishes Shelley's life and work weren't overshadowed quite so much by her earliest novel. Once or twice a year, students come into the library and claim they cannot find the copies of *Frankenstein*, and she takes them to the Shelley section and points out all the other novels. She tells them their lecturer will be hugely impressed if they reference these works as well. The students look at her as if she's saying, hey, why not do double the work for absolutely no reason?

'So? What happened?'

'I got a place, I just didn't get funding. I tried to save up for it. That was when I started working at the library, as a shelving assistant. I used to watch all the postgrads coming in and making these fortresses of books on their desks that I had to take to bits at the end of the night. I was saving, but it was really slow. I was living at home, I had to pay Mum board, and I had to get to the library, which was two buses each way.'

'You didn't have a *car*? I know you guys don't all have cars, but that sounds *terrible*.'

'Not really,' she says. 'If you can't afford it, you can't afford it.' Jerome asks if her parents didn't help, and she says that her mother couldn't, she'd never really worked so she didn't have much, and her father was living in the Cayman Islands.

'Right, so he was loaded.'

'If he was, he didn't share it with me. I wrote to him, a couple of times, but he never wrote back. Maybe the emails never reached him, I don't know. God, this is turning into a complete sob story, isn't it?'

'Oh, hey,' Jerome says, 'you wouldn't believe how many people have a sob story about the PhD they never got to do. My friend Clifton had to leave his programme in the second year because his Dad was basically drinking himself to death. It took four years for his liver to fail, and by then Cliff was completely out of the loop. His department wouldn't take him back. He's teaching high school now. He *hates* it.'

'Actually,' Claire says, 'I didn't think *Mathilda* was a minor work.'

'Oh, sure. I mean, it's still Mary Shelley.'

'Not just that.'

'What? You thought it was better than *Frankenstein*?' He's laughing. 'Look, it's fine, you do the minor works to get your funding, but this is what you gotta watch out for. It happens all the time. Grad students, the ones who don't have the guts to write on Picasso, they still wanna argue that their guy's just as good, even if they're the first person ever to publish on him, even if nobody else in the whole world agrees. They think it's that easy: you pick something small and make it big.'

Claire feels the stinging around her eyes again, the clenching in her throat. She grips the bench. 'I'd like a glass of wine now, please.'

Morning. She phones home, and Patience says, 'Do not worry, but your mother is feeling gloomy. She misses you, in her way.'

Claire's head is throbbing. It takes a moment for the news to filter through. 'She does?'

'It is only natural. You are her daughter, after all. Perhaps now the fact of your absence is properly sinking in for her.'

'Is she asking for me?'

'She is watching a lot of television.'

Claire hears a jingle from the bedroom: Jerome, fastening his jeans. She feels again the pressure of his gut in the night, his damp, hairless skin. She smells her own breath and remembers eating crispy pigs' ears in the pub.

'Let me talk to her,' she says.

It is not that she has never known her mother to be depressed. On the contrary: Jacqueline often has these slumps, in which she declares that life is not worth prolonging, that everything of value has already occurred. 'Dignitas,' she might say; or, occasionally, 'Rat poison.' These spells are not connected to the pain of arthritis, or the humiliations of old age, because Claire can remember a long phase of it that culminated in her coming home from school one winter's afternoon to find the house in darkness and her mother spreadeagled on the kitchen floor, apparently unconscious, possibly even dead: when she'd held her hand above the black crescent of her mouth, she'd felt no breath. It was only when Claire was phoning 999 that Jacqueline had opened her eyes. She'd waited until Claire noticed to actually speak ('More than two minutes that's taken you to call an ambulance. Do you *want* me dead?'), then risen triumphant, energised. She'd applied more lipstick by the time help arrived. 'You look just like Pierce Brosnan,' Claire heard her tell the paramedic. 'You do. Look at those eyes!'

Jacqueline gets to the phone and says, 'You have to come home. I can't take it any more. She's a nightmare. I think there's something wrong with her wiring. The other day she made a batch of scones and then fed them all to the birds! Some of my best face creams are missing.'

'She doesn't need face cream.'

'How do you know what she needs? We don't know anything about her. God knows what else she's got hidden in that suitcase. They might be selling them. They might have some sort of black market goods ring going. It's like being in a prison, Claire. You've put me in prison.'

Patience retrieves the phone. 'Claire, it is my assessment that your mother misses being able to affect you emotionally.'

'What do you mean? She misses talking to me?'

'It is not that she misses your company, or hearing your news. It is more that she misses being able to watch how you react to the things she says. I am not reactive. I'm like the television: it's all one-way.'

'But you talk to her, don't you?'

'Of course. We talk all the time.'

'Do you talk about me?'

'No.'

'Well, there's your answer,' Claire says with a gruesome laugh.

'What do you mean?'

'I mean you should try it. Try gossiping about me. She used to like doing that.' *With my brother*, she doesn't say. 'Maybe make the odd comment. See if it helps. You know: Claire's a bit bossy, or Claire didn't clean the oven very well. Maybe tell her I don't check in with you as much as your normal clients do.'

'But Claire, your level of contact is above average.'

'Just give her what you can.'

★

Towards the end of the fellowships, they are invited to give short presentations to the Institute on the work they've been doing. Claire attends Jerome's talk on *Covered Table with Pie* and is amazed at how authoritatively he discusses the likely provenance of this pie, the likely nature of the sauced and shining pulp of meat inside it, and how this connects to trade developments at the Vleeshal (literally *flesh hall*) at the Grote Market in town.

Claire's own presentation does not go well. She is reluctant to criticise Annika's project to her colleagues, but unwilling to praise it without foundation, and so her discussion turns out to be primarily descriptive; she begins to feel like Pieter Claesz, just painting what is there, never plunging beneath the surface. Even when she appears to speak analytically, to cut something open, it is only ever a simulation of openness, a staged exposure. The scholars present hardly pretend to applaud, and she is not offered a renewal of her fellowship for the following term.

Jerome's fellowship has not been renewed either, but he plans to stay in Europe for a few more weeks, avoiding home as long as he can. He will go to Berlin, then maybe to Rome; he will eat *schnitzel* and *cacio e pepe* and write up his presentation as a full-length article and send it out, because, 'Claire, I've gotta publish, or I'm stuck in Halla-bassee for ever.'

On Claire's last day, they meet at a coffee shop. Jerome insists on smoking a joint, though he never normally lets himself smoke in Haarlem: he says he'd never get anything done. Claire drinks her beer and watches his eyes droop.

'This is a sativa variety,' he says. 'It's much more mellow than the indicas. You sure you don't wanna try?'

'I'm fine.'

He breathes out a snake of pale smoke. 'You know,' he says, 'I'm gonna try and get back to Haarlem, or maybe Amsterdam, next summer. If I manage to swing something, you should come out and see me.'

Claire clamps her teeth together. The old pain leaps up. 'I'm my mother's primary carer,' she says, 'so we'll have to see. It depends how she's doing.'

'Who's looking after her now?'

Claire tells him about Patience. She explains her mother's unhappiness about the situation, her brother's unavailability to help. When she's finished, Jerome says, 'My father had a synthetic. He had dementia with Lewy bodies – which nobody's ever heard of, it's like the rarest thing – and all these calcium crystal diseases, where he had crystals building up in his joints, and gallstones, and stuff like that. He was deaf. I had to teach, I couldn't be home all the time, and he couldn't be left on his own. The synthetic was *great*. She just got on with it, no problem. She didn't care if he was yelling about home invaders or trying to show her his dick.'

'My mother's not like that.'

'I think it's amazing what you do. Absolutely amazing. I couldn't do it. I literally *could not do it.*'

'Don't you feel guilty?'

Jerome looks out of the window. Solemnly he says, 'My father passed. He was seventy-eight years old. And no, I wasn't there – but what I try to tell myself is, neither was he.'

They say goodbye on the pavement, an awkward hug, a promise to write. Then she goes back to her apartment and finishes packing. As she is dragging her bags down the stairwell, her phone buzzes with a text from the psychiatry museum: 'Hi Claire! Thank you for volunteering with us today! See you at 4pm!'

She is not in the mood, not in the slightest; she wishes bitterly she'd been called to volunteer earlier in her stay. Could she simply not go? She supposes she could. Other people flake out on their obligations. But Claire has always been dutiful. She will take her bags with her and ask to store them behind the desk. She will do this one last thing.

The compulsory chair has been removed from the main exhibition hall and placed in the former chancel for the Living Museum. It stands spotlit in the middle of the floor, the dramatic lighting making the burnished leather and the wooden wings shine. Claire swings her legs up on to the leg-rests and settles back. The spotlight closes her eyes.

'OK?' asks the museum assistant, Mikke, a bony young man with his hair slicked over to one side and a walkie–talkie crackling responsibly on his belt. He has already told her he will be there the whole time, and if she wants letting out, she only has to call his name. He has to say this for insurance reasons, just as he has to make her sign a waiver that will never be used.

'I'm gonna fasten the straps now, OK?'

'Then what do I do?'

'Whatever you like.'

'Do I talk to people?'

'If you like. Or go into your head. It's up to you.'

Not for a long time, she realises, once it begins, not for a very long time has she sat unoccupied like this – not working, not talking, not cooking or cleaning or reading, just sitting here. Occasionally people enter the room and circle around her, but she can't really see them; she can track their voices, but only if they are talking loudly enough, and even then, what they say is in Dutch. It isn't what she'd imagined – she'd imagined lying in the main exhibition hall, in daylight, laughing with other visitors who stopped to ask her what on earth she was doing. But maybe this is better. More eerie; more artistic.

She cannot see any part of the chair that supports her, or anything of the surrounding room except the doorway's square of light. It's like she's floating in the air. Her posture, it comes to her, is like the posture of someone being abducted by aliens in an old science fiction film, the body pulled upwards by the navel in a beam of light. But it isn't a beam of light that keeps her in position. It isn't the restraints, either. The chair is almost two centuries old, and she is afraid to damage it, so she lies very still. She doesn't even try to pull against the straps, to see how strong they are; she just stirs her body very slightly, now and then, to feel their pressure in place.

Shufflings and murmurings as a larger group enters the room. There's something expectant in the hush, and Claire is not surprised when a face rises above her, the silhouette of a face – an older woman's, her comb of pale hair backlit by the lights, and with something on her head, some strange contraption, a kind of silver disc.

'Miss Jansen,' the woman says, in an unidentifiable accent. 'What state are we in today?'

She is wearing a white jacket or coat, and carrying a clipboard that has the museum's logo on the back. Another volunteer, then. Or maybe an actor. Are there actors in the Living Museum?

'Afternoon rounds, Miss Jansen. Wakey-wakey. Is there anything you'd like to discuss?'

'I don't know,' Claire says, cautiously. The people in the room are quiet, presumably watching. 'What sort of thing?'

'Well. Yesterday you were telling me about your mother. Isn't that right?'

'My mother?'

'Yes.'

'I don't think I was.'

Someone makes a small coughing sound that might have been a nervous laugh.

'But it's here in my notes. It's right here. Your mother was a difficult woman, yes? She was very hard on you, yes? You told me about the yellow irises in the garden. How she cut them all down.'

'I didn't say that.'

'And sometimes you wished for bad things to happen to her, yes? You wished for bad things, and then she died and you thought it was your fault, because children think everything is always their fault.'

Is Claire hypnotised? Is that what this is? Because there is a memory unfolding in her, one she's never had before, of her mother on her knees in the garden with a pair of secateurs, and a row of stately irises snipped and toppling, one by one. Their petals, hearts and tongues, keep on quivering after they land.

'Isn't it a bit hackneyed to talk about mothers?' she says, and hears the woman smile. 'And a bit anachronistic to be using Freud on a patient from the 1850s?'

'I said it wasn't your fault – do you remember? I said it couldn't possibly be your fault, because you are not a supernatural being; you cannot make things happen just by wishing they would.'

'Obviously not.'

'Obvious to the grown-up. But you have to tell the child.'

'Oh my God. Who wrote this script?'

'When she becomes agitated,' says the woman, turning to address the room, 'Miss Jansen suffers from a very common delusion, which is that she is not really ill, she's just pretending to be ill. This is all a kind of performance. Allegedly, *I* have a script.'

The spectators laugh.

'Oh,' Claire says. 'And now we're postmodern. This really is a mess.'

They laugh a bit more.

'Maybe,' the woman says. 'Maybe you are very funny. But your resistance to talking about your mother seems significant to me. Do you feel that you betrayed her, somehow, by opening up to me yesterday?'

'Are you a volunteer?'

'In this delusion,' the woman explains, 'we are all visitors to a museum of psychiatry in which she has volunteered for a project. Ingenious, isn't it? I can't think of a better way to make yourself feel good about being stuck in here. What have you volunteered for this time?'

'Whatever it was, I'm starting to regret it.'

Nobody laughs at this, though Claire had meant to make a joke.

'*I'm starting to regret it*,' the woman repeats, with satisfaction. 'Do you see how important it is to you, to feel that you have *chosen* the compulsory chair? We can only regret the things we choose.'

'Fine,' Claire says. 'You're not a therapist. You're an inmate, just like me.'

'Very good! But I am free to roam the building,' the woman says, walking towards the doorway, 'and even to *leave* the building' – she returns – 'whereas you are confined.'

'I can leave. Any time I like. Mikke! Let me out!'

Finally, Patience has realised that Claire is not a saint. Of course from the outside it obviously looks that way. Obviously she has been caring for her mother. Jacqueline hasn't really gone hungry or dirty; she hasn't been left to the mercy of the council. But it's not as if Claire hasn't been getting anything out of it, wearing this homemade halo on her head.

'Caring,' says Patience, 'is something a person chooses to do.'

'She told me she wanted to look after me. What was I going to do, send her away? I mean, I could have. I did think about it. Maybe it would have been the best thing for her. It's not as if it's done her brother any harm. Ross, that's my son. He lives in Hong Kong now. He does something important for one of the banks there, I can't remember exactly what, but it's very, very important. He has to be out in Hong Kong. He can't be here.'

'You must be proud.'

'Must I? I don't really think about it. He was his own person, right from day one. You know he used to scream and scream about his swimming lessons? Oh my God, you've never heard such a voice. I'd got swimming lessons for the both of them and he *hated* it, so in the end I had to cancel them all. He's never liked the water. And now he lives on an island! It's just the way he is.'

Ross naked at the top of the stairs, throwing his trunks. Ross getting up from the table in the Golden Lotus, refusing to eat, refusing to stay, demanding the car keys so he could go and sit in the car. So much life in him! So much will!

'His father got to him. He had some way of keeping in touch, emails, messages, something like that. What can you do? A son needs a man around. When he was fifteen, he said he wanted to go out to the Caymans and see him. Oh, he was adamant! So I sent him, and he had the summer of his life, not that he thanked me for it. Alan was on his best behaviour. Boats and swimming and lobsters and all that kind of thing. Ross never wanted to leave, but of course his father wasn't going to keep him. He came home and he wouldn't settle. I wasn't surprised. He'd seen the world, hadn't he? I wasn't surprised he left when he did.'

'Claire has never mentioned her brother to me.'

'Of course she hasn't. He's living his life, she's living hers, but she takes it all so personally. Everything's *personal* with her.'

'She has felt for a long time that she is absolutely necessary to you. It will be difficult for her to come home and see that you have been fine.'

'I've been more than fine,' Jacqueline says irritably, and in that moment it does seem so to her, it does seem that the days in bed, the restless, dispirited viewing of the television, the tears, are just a bad dream. She has these dreams sometimes.

'Does Claire drink alcohol?' Patience asks.

'What a peculiar question.'

'Adult children of dependent parents are prone to depression when the parent dies or moves into a home. They are likely to turn to alcohol as a coping mechanism.'

'Oh, don't be ridiculous. Claire can't wait for me to die. She'll probably pop the champagne.'

'That's what I'm worried about.'

'Patience!' Jacqueline exclaims, with a fierce pleasure that surprises even her. 'You made a joke!'

When Claire drops her bags and bends down for a kiss, her mother says, 'You stink of weed. Is that what you've been doing all this time?'

Jacqueline is bright and upright in her chair, her blouse clean and pressed. The house is spotless. Calla lilies glow like heliodor on the windowsill.

'*I've* been working,' Jacqueline says. 'I'm writing my memoirs. It was all Patience's idea. I was telling her my stories, and unlike you she seemed to think they were amusing – she said, why don't you write them down? So I've started to write them down. I'm writing about your father, as a matter of fact.'

The storm, or whatever it was, seems to have passed. Perhaps it passed the moment Claire called and said she was coming home. She brings out her desultory airport gifts, some wax-wrapped cheese, some playing cards, a packet of Stroopwafel, while Jacqueline says, 'You won't remember this, but he once took us up in a private pod on the London Eye and gave me a diamond bracelet.'

'You're right: I don't remember.'

'What're those? Are they caramel? I don't like caramel. It glues all my teeth together. Do *you* eat them? Oh Claire, you'll look older than *me*! Your father looked older than he was. People thought I was his child!'

They eat dinner together from trays in the living room, fish and chips and tartar sauce weedy with dill, everything homemade, while Patience crouches on the floor and polishes the gas fire's fender.

'Isn't she a wonder? However did we manage without her? I suppose it's being a machine, isn't it? You just do everything *perfectly*. There's no human error. Do you remember that bolognese you made, Claire? When you put *cinnamon* in it?'

'Mum, we need to talk about this.'

'God Almighty, I'll never understand! What would possess anyone to put *cinnamon* in spaghetti bolognese?'

'I looked after you. I was here twice a day. That's going to have to be good enough again.'

Her mother scrapes her knife along her plate. 'Who's going to wash all the floors? She gets them so *clean*!'

'What happened to feeling like you were in prison?'

'Oh Claire, where do you *get* these things? Patience, don't listen. I never said that.'

'You did,' Patience says. 'I heard it.'

'Bollocks,' Jacqueline replies.

'Patience, can you give us a minute?'

Patience goes into the kitchen, where she starts clattering the dishes around. Is she always this noisy? Or is she clattering for effect, pretending to be hurt? Who told her she could do that?

'Mum, surely you can see there's no need for us to keep her on now I'm home? Surely you don't want me wasting money?'

'She's been a great comfort to me, you know. She's been an angel.'

'But none of it's real. She's not *real*.'

'Oh, I see. When you're off on your holidays, she's fine, she's marvellous, but now you're back she isn't good enough? She's more use than *you*, I can tell you that.'

Claire doesn't answer, and Jacqueline adds, 'Patience thinks you'll go mad if you're not in charge of me any more.'

'Patience tells you what you want to hear.'

'She says you'll turn to the drink. You'll become an alcoholic.'

Whatever the language of rebuttal would be, Claire cannot find it. Her head is flooded with a roaring white noise. Her face feels numb.

'Don't stare. You look moronic. Your father was a drinker, did you know that? He beat your brother once, black and blue. I've never understood how he forgave him for it.'

'Yes,' Claire says, 'it's amazing, since he never forgave *you*.'

She thinks it's a stinging blow, but her mother smiles. She settles back down like a cat that's finished licking its paws.

'I'm calling them,' Claire says. 'I'm ending the contract.'

'Fine,' says Jacqueline. 'I'll just pay for her myself. What else am I doing with my estate?'

'Your *estate*? This house and two ratty fur coats nobody wants, that's your estate.'

'Listen to her! Did you leave your manners in France? You don't know everything about me, Claire Marie. Maybe I won the lottery. How would *you* know? Maybe Grandad squirrelled something away before the crooks got it all. Maybe I took more than you realise off your father in the divorce.'

'Mum,' Claire says, with sudden misgiving, 'you can't remortgage the house.'

'I'd never do that.'

Wouldn't she? Claire has no idea. It's only the lack of anger, the lack of shiftiness, in Jacqueline's expression that finally gives her a curious, settling sensation of belief. She believes what her mother is saying. The conjunctivitis, she notices, has gone.

'You've got money,' she says.

'I've got enough.'

After six weeks in the Haarlem apartment, Claire is dismayed by the state of her own flat. The piles of boxes no longer pass for furniture. Pink mould blooms on the bathroom wall. She crawls into bed but she can't fall asleep. Is this what it's like to be Patience – never off, always on? Or her mother, even? Her mother hardly sleeps, she likes to claim. There's no relief for either of them, she thinks. No relief from being what they are.

The money, too, keeps biting into her thoughts. Where did it come from? And when? If her mother's had it since the divorce, then she had it the whole time Claire was saving for the PhD. She remembers all the discouraging comments, the swipes at the ivory tower; she remembers her mother totting up what was owed. It can't be that. It has to be more recent. But her mother doesn't have any friends any more, no relatives to speak of. How has she come across it? And this is the little glowing seed in it all, the bit Claire wants to hold on to, because the only person she can think of is Ross. Ross making all that money in Hong Kong. Getting older, finally. Sending something home.

Patience would know. Claire could ask her, and she'd tell the truth. But if Claire asked, she would have to hear the answer. She lets this prospect drift, and instead imagines writing a letter. It would have to be a real letter: Ross is too high up in the company for his email address to be public. She would thank him for the money. She would say that it enabled her mother to secure a synthetic carer who is making

her life, and Claire's, much easier now. She would tell him she
has recently undertaken a fellowship in Europe that would
not have been possible without his generosity. She would
show him he'd been wrong – she wasn't trapped. If the money
was his, he'd be flattered; if not, he might be embarrassed
into reaching out and correcting the mistake. She falls asleep
drafting the letter in her mind, and dreams of Ross in the bus
station holding a bouquet of yellow balloons.

Claire stopped paying for Patience, and Patience remained.
Life had a different rhythm now. Claire still visited her mother
after work, and sometimes in the mornings, too, but it wasn't
required. They ate together. Patience cooked. Afterwards,
the dishes were gleaming, the hobs wiped, the counters bare.
Patience had even put the tea towel in the wash and hung
a clean one from a hook. The bird feeders, then – Claire
could fill those. She got the sack of seed and went out on to
the patio, but of course the feeders were already replenished,
a shower of kernels on the flags beneath. Or had she done
it herself already? Had she spilled? The sacks were always
splitting.

'Here,' said Patience, coming up behind her, 'why don't
you just relax? I have brought you another glass of wine.'

It was her mother's Chardonnay. Patience had been order-
ing extra bottles and stowing them in the garage, on the cold
stone floor. Even the glass was chilled.

'You think of everything,' Claire said. 'I suppose you
know what I'm going to do next.'

'No, Claire. Nobody knows that.'

'But you could guess?'

'Of course. You have challenged me to predict your behaviour, which means you will probably do something deliberately unpredictable, such as eating a handful of birdseed off the ground.'

'Wrong! I'm going to finish this glass of wine.'

Claire drank it, fast. A cold hand reached down her throat and into her stomach. Patience watched with what seemed like disapproval.

'Oh relax,' Claire said. 'It's Friday. Everyone's having a drink. It's what we do.'

She sat down on the bench from which her mother watched the birds when the weather was good. There were no birds around now, obviously. It was night-time, getting late. Probably she would sleep here, in the spare room. She had done that a few times lately, getting Patience to make up the bed. Her own flat was depressing. Even the mattress felt damp.

'Patience?'

'Yes?'

'That suitcase you brought with you. What have you got in there?'

It was obvious once she'd framed the question, even before Patience replied. Nothing. There was nothing in the case. Patience had just carried it to seem more human when she first arrived.

THE MAN IN ROOM SIX

I knocked gently. When there was no reply, I knocked again.

'Come in ...' An English voice.

I clamped the hot water bottle under my arm and opened the door. It was gloomy in there, one lamp shining weakly under a flowered shade. The man was lying down, though not completely: his shoulders and head were propped against the headboard. He was wearing a collared shirt and tie. His legs were stretched out in front of him. He still had his shoes on. My mother would have told him to take them off.

'Who's this, then?' the Englishman said. 'I was expecting your Mum. She is your Mum, isn't she?'

I nodded.

'Yes, I see it now. Come in a bit. You've got the hair, haven't you? The red hair.'

I didn't like the way he said *the red hair*, but I still hadn't given him the things he'd rung for, the hot water bottle and the glass of ice, which my mother had told me to fetch without making a nuisance of myself. He gave no sign of rising, so I went to the foot of the bed. I could see him better now. His face was soft and toady, and his grey hair needed cutting.

'That's it,' he said, 'into the light. Well, you're a bonny thing, aren't you? That's what you say up here, isn't it? "Bonny"?'

'I suppose.'

'Oh, you suppose? Well, I think you do. I think I've heard it. My mother was from these parts, you know. Don't look so surprised,' he said, though I wasn't. 'I know, you wouldn't think it to listen to me. Sound like a right Sassenach, don't I?'

I held the items towards him.

'Oh, you're in a rush, are you? Everyone's in a rush these days, aren't they? But what have you got to get back to? A cartoon you're watching? Some homework? God, for the days when all I had to worry about was a bit of homework!'

He gave a clogged sort of laugh and moved slightly, and the smell of my father in the mornings reached me: whisky and unwashed dressing gown.

'All right,' he said, 'all right, just put that here.'

I went right up and put the glass of ice on the nightstand. I gave the hot water bottle to him, and he sighed as he took hold of it.

'Such a simple thing,' he said. 'Such a simple pleasure.' And he placed it on his stomach.

I asked, as my mother had told me to, 'Is there anything else you need?'

'No, no, this is it. Just reach us that bottle, would you?'

He pointed past me into the shadows. I turned and saw the whisky bottle on the desk. It was half-full. I picked it up and took it to him.

'Just pour us a bit in there,' he said, pointing to the glass.

'With all the ice?'

'Listen to you! What do you know about ice?'

'My Dad doesn't like it.'

'Oh yes? And why not?'

I felt I had already said too much, but the Englishman was watching me eagerly.

'He says it's sacrilege.'

I thought he might be angry, but he laughed. He seemed delighted. 'Sacrilege! Listen to her! Do you know what that means?'

'Yes.'

'Go on, then. What does it mean?'

'It means spoiling something.'

'Spoiling,' he said, thoughtfully. 'Yes, I suppose it does.' Then he brightened again. 'Trust a Scot to turn his whisky into a religious experience!'

I felt a bit offended on my father's behalf, and said, 'Actually, he takes it very seriously.'

'Oh, I bet he does,' the Englishman said. 'I bet he's got the sanctimonious bit down pat. Do you know what *that* means? "Sanctimonious"?'

I shook my head.

'It means you think you know better than everyone else. God, and why wouldn't you? If I'd got a place like this, and a girl like you, hanging on my every word, I'd think the same way. I'd think, look at this precious life, look how amazing she thinks I am! Pour a bit in there, would you? Yes, I want the ice, I don't care.'

The cork came out of the bottle with a hollow pop. I must have poured too much, because he said, 'Steady on,' and reached out to knock the bottle away.

'Sorry,' I said.

'That's all right, that's all right. You'll do better next time, won't you?'

He had to tuck his chin into the soft folds of his neck to reach the rim of the glass, and this movement made the folds spread wider, covering the knot in his tie. He put the glass's rim to his lips and tilted it slowly. I heard the whisky draining through the ice, through his teeth, and the suck of his tongue at work as he rolled it around his mouth. When he swallowed, the liquid trickled down through his complicated chest, and when it reached his belly, it made an angry bubbling sound.

'Hang on,' he said, as I began to withdraw. 'Hang on. I've got a question for you. Why don't you sit? Just for a minute.'

I thought of my mother in the kitchen, cutting the break-fast scones. If she realised I had been upstairs this long, she would collar me in the hall when I came back down and say, *Have you got nothing better to do that you've got to go bothering people? Do you need a job?* But I wasn't bothering the English-man, that was the truth, and in fact it seemed like it would bother him more if I left. I sat on the edge of the armchair beside the window. The curtains were not drawn, and I could feel the cold air seeping through the glass and breathing on the back of my head.

'Tell me,' he said. 'Have you got any boys you love?'

This startled me. I didn't know how to answer.

'Of course you haven't,' he said. He took another sip of his whisky. 'You're too young for all that nonsense. But it's coming, isn't it? It's coming.' He gestured at the window. 'Spring's coming. You sure there isn't a boy you've got your eye on?'

I frowned. There was a boy, but the Englishman surely couldn't know it.

'Oh, so there is,' he said, and gave his thick laugh again.

'No,' I said. 'There's not.'

'Right you are. Right you are.' He tapped his nose and winked. Then he sighed and seemed to settle deeper into the bed.

'Do me a favour, though,' he said. 'Do me a favour. When there *is* a boy you like, you have to tell him. Do you know why?'

I shook my head.

As if it was painful to him, he said, 'Because it's a kindness.'

I thought he was going to say more, but he went quiet for a minute, resting the glass of whisky on top of the hot water bottle on his stomach. I felt the cold on the back of my head again.

'They don't know themselves,' he went on after a moment. 'But you know. You see them. And you have to tell them. Imagine if he'd been told – what it would have been. It's a kindness. Do you get what I'm saying? Even if he doesn't like you back, you'll have given him something that he'll carry with him through his whole life. That someone saw him, and they wanted him. That's so precious. And you've got the power to do that. Do you see what I mean? You've got that power, and you don't even know it. Look at you – God! And you don't even have to be beautiful – you just have to be what you are, and he'll thank you for it.' He hoisted himself back up on one elbow, leaning towards me, slopping his drink, and said, with fierce urgency, 'Promise me.'

I said, 'I promise.'

That seemed to calm him. He sank back down on the bed again. His glass was tipped at an angle on top of the water bottle. I waited for him to right it, but he didn't, so I nipped forward to straighten it for him before it spilled completely.

'That's a love,' he said. His eyes were closing. His grip was loose. I was scared to take the glass away from him, but I didn't trust him to keep hold of it by himself. We both touched it for a moment. Then I eased it away and set it back on the nightstand.

'That's a love,' he said again. He mumbled something I didn't catch. His eyes were completely closed now, and I could study his face, the soft pink warty growth beside his nose, the grease of his hair where it swept back at his temples. Then his eyes flared open, and I coughed in fright.

'In the bathroom,' he said. 'There's a bottle of perfume. On the shelf. Would you bring it here? I've kept you too long, I know . . .'

In the bathroom there was a glint coming off the glass shelf over the sink, and I reached for it, but instead of a perfume bottle I touched something like tinfoil that rustled at my fingertips. I reached up higher and tugged the cord of the shaving light. It sprang on, horribly bright, and I saw how the glass shelf was covered in empty foil blister packs. Some of them had fallen off into the sink. The bottle of perfume, a tall thin cone of frosted glass, stood right at the shelf's end, with something Japanese printed on it and a silver atomiser at the top. The plastic tube that fed the atomiser only just touched the last drop of perfume left in the base of the glass. I carried the bottle to the Englishman and put it in his hands as if he was blind.

'There's a girl, there's a girl,' he said. 'That's the one. But you take it. You spray a bit – just there, on your wrist. You'll like the smell. It's a beautiful smell.'

I knew it was wrong of him to ask me. It was wrong of me to have stayed this long already. I was troubled by the empty packets in the bathroom, by the whisky, by the slackness of his face.

'No,' I said. 'I'd better not.'

'Just a little test,' he said. 'Like in the shops. You like to try the perfumes out, don't you?'

'No, thank you.'

'Please? *Please.*' He pushed the bottle towards me, and I took it. 'There's a girl, now. There's a love. On your wrist.'

I got it by the atomiser and held out my arm. I pressed. There was a tiny hiss, a fine cold spray: I felt it touch me before I smelled it, but the smell came soon after, drift-ing upwards from the bottle and then, as it warmed, from my skin. It was a smell of things I couldn't name, though I went through myself looking for them. I thought of the raspberries my father grew in the garden in summer, the sourness that squirted from the plastic lemon in the kitchen cupboard, the bath foam my mother liked. None of them smelled like this.

The Englishman sighed. 'Closer,' he said. 'Come a bit closer there.'

I leaned even closer, and his hand came up and touched me just beneath the elbow. His fingernails had ridges running through them, as if they had been folded. Very gently he guided my wrist towards his face. 'Isn't it beautiful? Just the most beautiful smell.'

'It's really nice.'

'Christ, it isn't *nice*. It's gorgeous. It's wild! And your skin – you know everyone's skin has a different smell?'

He had brought my wrist so close to his face that I could feel his warm breath, the stubble on his lip, the hairs poking from his nose.

'This on you, it's … lighter somehow. And warm. Like cinnamon, or … God, what was that cake we used to get?' His voice was faint now, his lips hardly moving. His hand relaxed on to his chest. His chin dropped slightly. The bulb of his nose pressed against my wrist bone. Softly I gave a little push, and watched his head tip back and settle against the pillow.

I left the room, shutting the door as quietly as I could, and crept towards the stairs. My mother would have noticed my absence by now. She would be scrubbing the mixing bowl with her head tipped to one side, as if she were listening to the scones rise in the oven, when really she was listening for me. I would have to wash the perfume off before she smelled it.

On the landing there was a big picture window, and I paused beside it, looking out across the silvery loch. The moon was small and hard and bright. I lifted my wrist to my face.

WITH THEM INTERCEDE
FOR US ALL

She was drunk, okay, there's no arguing with that; but sober enough to take her bracelet off. It was on the floor later. That's what she can't forget. The metal bracelet, silver-plated, solid links, a snap she prised open. Fiddly. Then she put it on the bedside table. So it wouldn't hurt her in her sleep.

★

When she gets off the plane she's waiting for the hot air to meet her, holiday air, like opening the oven door, but it doesn't. It's end of season, and the sky is as grey as the sky she left behind. Down the metal steps on to the airstrip. No tunnel. Everything exposed. She sees men unloading luggage from the belly of the plane – she sees them toss the bags into a plastic skip, thumping and crash-ing, dead weights, jumbled up. She doesn't see the yellow lines painted on the ground. Someone has to show her to the door.

For a minute in the arrivals hall she thinks Demetra hasn't remembered. She stands apart from the crowd, looking. Her breath comes with an audible fight. Not now. Not here. The inhaler's in her jacket – she fishes it out. Then the crowd splits and Demetra steps forward, smiling, with a red cotton braid in her hair.

'You stay tonight in Athens,' Demetra tells her in the car. 'The boat is very early in the morning or late in the afternoon. I thought you would want to sleep.'

'I would,' she says, 'thank you,' but she's wired from the plane.

Demetra lives in Kaisariani, on a comparatively quiet street. When Claire climbs out of the car she feels particles of dust break over her in a wave and enter her body, closing her throat. She bends double with one hand on the warm side panel. There are dark tracks in the dust on the road. The inhaler's in her hand and this time she needs it. Click and breathe – click and breathe. The tracks are from Demetra's tyres. They must have driven through water on their way.

The apartment is on the third floor above a pharmacy. Demetra leads her in silence down the dark hall into the living room and closes the living room door. 'Yiannis is sleeping,' she says. 'I know. I know. But I can't deal with him. It's better this way.' When they laugh they laugh with their hands across their mouths.

★

Hotel Oceanis. The name means nothing. She looked it up on Wikipedia. No matches: nothing spelled that way. There was a Titan called Oceanus, whom Zeus folded into the earth along with all the rest. Oceanus had daughters, the Oceanids – Sibelius wrote some music about them. The name could be a corruption of that. But she thinks it was specious. She thinks it was meant to sound good, to sound Greek. To reassure the tourists that they were in the right place.

★

She wakes in Demetra's sister's room, under a cliff of trinket-laden shelves, to the sound of women's voices. In the kitchen, Demetra says, 'Claire, this is my mother. Tell her *chronia pola* – many years. It's her name day. Saint Sofia's day.' Claire says it. Somehow the words sound right. '*Brava!*' cries Sofia, who has stopped by with a brown paper bag full of bread from church. The bread is good luck. Claire takes a piece. It's sour and yeasty, breaking apart before it even touches her mouth. Then Sofia presses a postcard into her hands: Saint Sofia in a bright green gown, the patron of wisdom, standing tall behind her three daughters: Pistis, Elpis, Agape.

It is comforting to sit on the balcony and listen to them chatter in words she doesn't understand. It is comforting to watch the acacia leaves, greyish-green, piled like clouds, and the balconies they cover, balconies like this one, tiny private boxes hung above the street. After a while she lets her eyes drop to the pavement where citizens walk. She studies their faces. *Not him . . . Not him . . .*

Demetra drives her out to Piraeus. They stop across the road from gate 62. There is a central reservation full of red dianthus past its best, then the massive wire fence and the fortified gate, and beyond that a world of concrete: huge ramps, many levels, realms of parking, all pearly grey, and the ghosts of ships in the distance that look too large to float.

'Are you sure you'll be alright?' Demetra asks. Claire wants to tell her; then she doesn't. 'I'll be fine,' she says. 'I've been there before.' They hug awkwardly across the gear stick. 'See you soon.' 'See you soon.'

From the rail she watches the port recede. She watches the white wake that the boat lays behind itself, seething and violent, then a different blue. It lasts too long. She takes the silver bracelet from her bag and puts it on.

The boat calls at twelve different islands. Hers is the sixth. It comes round quicker than she thought it would, after only four hours, gathering form at the edge of the sea. She feels like they're sailing up a waterfall. This is the lip, the rock on the lip that breaks the waters just before they drop. The rock is white and intricate as coral. Its ridges turn to rows of painted houses. Soon they are backing into the harbour: the turbines get louder the slower they go. Ropes fly down. Gates unlatch. Dots of people watch from the promenade as Claire and a handful of others disembark. The gangplank rolls beneath her feet, but the air is fresh and her breath doesn't catch.

She is sitting in a square, at a small metal table that tilts on the cobbles. The *kyria* who serves her is elderly, her hair dyed red in faded curls. She brings Claire strong coffee and asks where she is staying. 'Hotel Oceanis.' The *kyria* frowns. She tells her that Oceanis is closed down, finished. She chops with her hand. Claire should stay at Hotel Maria. It's her sister's place. It's very nice. 'But when did it close? Has it been knocked down?' The *kyria* says, no, Oceanis is still there, making a face. It closed three years ago. 'How do I get there?' She starts to wipe around the empty glass, around the ashtray. She says Oceanis is nothing, it's old, nobody looks after it, nobody cares about it. She shakes the cloth. She sighs. 'Two kilometres south on the main road.'

It's a steep climb out of the village on the narrow road that follows the island's spine, rising and rising. The island is long and thin. At one point she can see blue water on both sides of her, far below, rubbing against the rocks.

The earth is unremittingly baked and bare. Ancient terraces lurch down the slopes. She passes a house of white-washed stones where a cultivated fig tree thrusts its dark dusty leaves through the fence. Around its base fallen figs rot in the black shade.

She crests a rise, and there is the access road on the left. She remembers the sign. It was made of moulded fibreglass and buxom as a ship's figurehead, some kind of watery female creature, welcoming every guest with a wink. The sign is still there, but faded now, and long seeded grasses have grown up around it. Tumbleweeds make a draught-excluder along the bottom rail of the locked gates. No climbing them, but the wall is low, and when she walks its perimeter, towards the sea, she finds a place where creepers have forced the stones apart and sent them cascading to the ground. She scrambles over. The stones knock beneath her feet.

*

She was drunk, okay, there's no arguing with that. Sweet retsina burned in the hollow of her throat. Jane was drunk too but she looked well for it. They matched each other glass for glass, miserable Claire, brilliant Jane. Is that right? Jane in her gingham dress and canvas shoes with thick rubber heels. Beetle-crushers, they called them. The pool made flickering lights in the air, spooky green in the greenish wine, and she drank it all, till her body seemed to burn and ripple like the spotlit water did. When they poured again she drank that too.

*

Here is the half-moon terrace by the pool. She remembers a rail where long-legged women leaned, in gold-hooped earrings and cut-out costumes, their wayfarers filtering the dazzle off the sea. Blue-headed lizards basked in the light of the manager's gold buttons. They frightened her in the bathrooms, jittering from tile to tile, like pieces in a board game that followed no obvious rules.

Now the pool is dry and full of dust. She walks its perimeter, past a few white plastic sunloungers, all of which are coated in a film of grey but otherwise unchanged. These imperishable things. She stands where she thought their table once stood, the table where they sat and drank. In the pool, the spotlights are broken. Tough little herbs have sprouted up between the blue tiles.

At the edge of the terrace, half the rail has fallen away, the metal rusted and sheared. Nobody has blocked the gap. The ground simply ends, giving out into blue. She walks closer, passing a tall yellow flower that scratches her bare calf. She can hear the sea. It is still down there, though nothing else is, asking the same questions it asked of itself eighteen years before.

Two sunloungers have blown through the glass wall that separated the terrace from the restaurant. She steps through the hole, minding her legs, into cavernous, echoing shade. This is where they sat every morning for pots of Greek yoghurt and honey, in the evening for moussaka, kalamari, ice cream. The tables and chairs and long service trestles are gone now, and the folding stage where the singer or comedian or balalaika-player once stood. The red parquet floor is strewn with bits of glass and splinters. After the performance, the furniture would be stacked away for people to dance. Free-standing disco lights flashed on either side of the stage, weak splashes of red and blue on the faces of wrinkled ladies, emergency lights on the surface of the sea.

★

Pistis, Elpis, Agape. She looked up the story in the guidebook on the boat. All of them were killed by Hadrian's soldiers, one by one, in chronological order.

★

In the corner of the restaurant is the bar where Kostas shook cocktails and flicked the caps off bottles of Mythos. It is painted green on the customer side, raw plywood on the reverse. The fridges and the optics are gone. Claire presses her toe into the ringed indentation left on the floor by a bar stool's fixture. She remembers climbing carefully on to those high leatherette seats, the poles wobbling in their brackets. How afraid she had been of looking like a fool.

Kostas was the owner's youngest son. He worked in the restaurant at night. He had a deep tan and a deep voice, but he was only twenty, and his chest was reassuringly naked where it showed at the neck of his shirt. On the second night, he presented Jane with a virgin cocktail from the bar – tequila sunrise without the tequila. Jane's parents chose to be amused by this rather than concerned, and Claire thought she might admire Jane for that, for having such parents, more than for having the cocktail itself.

After his shift, Kostas did not simply go home, like an English waiter would. He stuck around. He liked to smoke outside on the terrace. Jane and Claire met him there. How regular it seemed, for just a week's routine. Jane accepted the pure white cigarettes he drew with his lips from their packet.

'You don't smoke?' he said to Claire. 'Everybody smokes in Greece.' Much of his talk consisted of explaining to the girls what it was like to be Greek: 'There are no jobs but also no McDonalds', or 'We close up and sleep for the afternoon', or 'When we argue, we argue about parking our cars.'

Jane laughed every time Kostas offered Claire a cigarette. Maybe that was why he kept doing it. Eventually Jane said, 'It won't work. She's good. My parents think she's a good influence on me.' It hung in the air with the smoke.

★

I used to be good, she thinks to herself, walking down the corridor away from the restaurant. She takes the inhaler from her pocket and administers a breath. Everything is tiled to repel heat. The walls are painted hospital white. *I used to be good.* But goodness only belongs to the young. You might not lose it, exactly, but after a point it becomes something else much duller, much less commendable. The asthma, for example. Not smoking because you don't want to is one thing, but then they diagnose the asthma and it's nothing heroic after all. Jane would have laughed. *All those years not smoking, you've got asthma anyway.*

At the end of the corridor is the lobby, the massive check-in desk bolted to the floor, the rep's clipboard and paperwork gone. Beyond the lobby are the rooms.

She thinks she will know which room was hers, but she doesn't. All the internal doors have been removed: each space opens to her view as she passes, like the pigeonholes at work, and she cannot tell one from another. She loses count.

Her room was number fifteen. She was fifteen at the time. They both were. They noticed the coincidence. Jane found an obscure satisfaction in taking the older room. Fifteen, sixteen. The markers were important. Now Claire forgets.

★

Martyrs must also be young. But how do the young know what they have to lose? What does that kind of martyrdom mean, when your eyes are half-closed? Even Sofia – she was a full-grown woman, yes, but it was her daughters she saw destroyed. Who can judge the sacrifice?

★

They sat on the terracotta-tiled patio outside their rooms and spoilt their dinner with Cheetos. They talked about Kostas. 'Do you really think he likes me?' Jane would ask, her neediest hour, and Claire had no choice but to say, yes, I think he does. Underneath the beach towel slung over her shoulders, Jane wore a red bikini with a frill round the edge. Claire could not imagine anything more daring than a red bikini. She had a navy one-piece that squashed her breasts against her ribs, and she changed back into cut-off jeans immediately after swimming.

She liked Kostas too, there's no denying that, but when she asked him to make her a tequila sunrise he narrowed his eyes and said, 'Sure', and forgot to put a cherry in it.

A virgin tequila sunrise is orange juice with grenadine. The syrup soaked upwards through the glass as they watched, like blood unravelling in toilet water. 'Weird,' Kostas said. 'It's called grenadine, but it's red.'

★

She enters a room whose angles seem familiar. There are holes in the walls where the storage has been ripped away. The tiny cubicle bathroom is also gutted. Only the splashbacks are left, and ugly plugholes in the floor and the walls, like nostrils without a nose. At the end of the room, the sliding glass patio doors are ablaze with light.

The patio is as she remembers it, small, not private, its view blocked by a grove of olive trees. She sits on the low wall. Since the walk down the long dusty corridor, she has not reached for her inhaler. She does not feel anxious at all. There are memories here, but she has brought them with her. Nothing new occurs. Nothing is dislodged.

★

It was cold, at night, on the terrace. Bumps rose on her arms and legs, and she drank partly to obliterate this, to forget her flesh and the terrible ease with which Jane inhabited her own body. The plastic chair bit sharp ridges in Claire's thighs. Even this discomfort had faded by the time Nikos appeared, and, with a sudden grand swell of sociability, she welcomed him into the group, making room at the table, dragging up a chair.

He was already drunk. His and Kostas's cigarettes burnt orange holes in the night, drew legible swirls like sparklers. Somewhere downhill a donkey cranked out its miserable cry. Claire's breath grew scratchy, a wheeze she could hide at first, until it made her cough: a deep, rasping note, a masculine distress. The boys looked at one another in amazement. '*Yitharos!*' Kostas exclaimed, and Nikos shouted with laughter. Kostas spoke to Jane and Jane laughed too. Claire's face inflamed. She didn't know for sure what it meant, she told herself.

★

Movement among the olive trees: a woman. She comes closer. She has not seen Claire yet. Small and bent, dressed all in black, she drags something black behind her – a net. The whole grove of trees is swagged in black nets, like the nets inside the rigging of a circus tent, to catch the olives when they fall.

The woman stops under the trees. Now she sees Claire: she turns, a hand to her brow. Then she unleashes a flock of Greek words that fly from the grove towards the deserted hotel building. Claire sees some of them catch in the nets, catch in the netted branches of the trees, all the spiky Greek letters unfolded – upsilon, theta, gamma, psi – staggering towards her. She is suddenly aware of herself as a trespasser, and she holds up her hands in a gesture of surrender. The woman slashes with her arm. Claire steps off the patio and hurries away from her, away from her torrent of indecipherable words, down the path that will take her to the terrace and the wall she climbed and the road and the nautical girl.

Jane would have stayed and talked, she thinks. Jane would not have run away. And she realises that this feeling of panic, this feeling of getting into trouble, is familiar, is left over, from her time in Jane's orbit.

★

She was in bed and the bed was rolling, a raft on a swollen sea. It was all she could do to cling on. She had been sick: some of it hung in her hair like spray. The sea was green and bioluminescent. She was hundreds of miles from land, miles, even, from the ocean floor. She could hear the thumping of a helicopter far off. They were looking for her but she could not move. Every so often the searchlights washed across her, without stopping – or else it was a wave, bearing in its body thousands of luminous creatures, sweeping them over the raft, leaving her behind.

★

She walks back down the main road towards the town. When she is halfway between the windmill and the house with the fig tree, on a stretch of road with nothing either side but low scrubby grasses and the white dots of shrines, she hears a loud buzzing by the right side of her head. She waves it away, but it comes closer, and then, when she thinks it can get no louder, it enters her ear.

She shrieks, and the shriek sounds far away compared to the drill-bit buzzing inside her. She tips her right ear downwards, hoping the thing will drop out, but it is determined to go deeper, against the pull of gravity. It is small and hard. Some kind of beetle, she thinks, bracing nevertheless for a sharpness, a sting. She wonders if she should flip her head over the other way, if it would climb towards the light, but she cannot stand the prospect, and stays where she is.

There is a long, lonely minute where she dwindles to the radius of her earhole and can think only of tweezers and hospitals and pincers and legs and her loneliness up here, her total loneliness, nobody to look at it, nobody to draw it out.

The creature makes a decision of its own and withdraws as quickly as it came, so quickly she catches only a flash of green iridescence as it whirs off across the dry scrub towards the horizon. The world is explosively large again. She crouches in the dust at the side of the road and sobs with horror and relief.

*

There was a knock and it seemed important to answer it. She staggered upright in her short pyjamas to the door, but nobody was there. The knock came again, from the patio. She drew the curtain back. Kostas and Nikos were outside. They smiled at her, and then their smiles vanished, and then they returned. She was trying to understand why they were there. She felt obscurely flattered. What did they want?

She lifted the latch and the door flew out of her hand, sideways, slamming back on its runners, and the two of them were in the room, the curtain was billowing, she was falling back on to her narrow single bed and they were falling with her, all three of them on the bed now, fingers in her hair. She laughed. She was waiting, it seemed to her later, for the thing to start – whatever they had come to do.

★

The last time she saw Jane was five years ago. At least, she thinks it was Jane. Claire was home for Christmas, home to her mother's house, and she walked a long way down the coast on Boxing Day, the hours having expanded to an intolerable size, almost the size of Sundays as a child, when noise and playing were forbidden. She was high on the path, hugging the cliffs, watching the grey English sea wet the shingle, when she saw a woman below her, at sea level, a woman alone, struggling to make real progress through the stones, walking slowly, half-sinking to the side. Ropes of kelp caught around her feet. It was madness to walk on the beach instead of the path. She looked mad. She also looked like Jane. Claire had thought for a moment about scrambling down to meet her, or at least to make sure, but the thought was gone almost as soon as it occurred, and she found that she had turned back all of a sudden, turned as sharply as the wind could turn, from front to back, from help to hindrance.

★

Hotel Maria is a stone-built two-storey house covered in flowerless waxy networks of bougainvillea. The *kyria* who books her in is undoubtedly Maria: she has the same faded red hair as her sister. Perhaps the colour was genuine after all; or perhaps they are so close that they share their henna. She imagines them painting their curls on a Sunday night. 'Your luggage?' Maria asks, pointing at Claire's small rucksack. 'Yes,' says Claire. 'I'm not staying long.' Her voice sounds strange. She can still feel the buzzing, the memory of it. She pays for one night in advance.

Her room has bumpy walls that are smoothly plastered white, a gold saint's portrait above the bed, and blue shutters that let her look down into the square. She drops her bag on the bed and props her postcard against the mirror. Saint Sofia: is she, then, a saint because she had to watch it happen?

There is a well in the centre of the square, and a plane tree peeling in jigsaw pieces, and two tavernas, one open, one shut. She watches a skinny cat circle the well twice then stroll towards the taverna that is open, weaving between the legs of the drinkers outside: men demolishing little glass bottles of ouzo; a couple with bread and wine. She settles herself at a table under the plane tree, among the shed pieces of its bark, and the skinny cat comes to skim her ankles. Its ears are tatty from fighting. When she rubs its head she feels the pits of fleabites against the little skull.

'You can feed her,' says an English voice. Claire looks up. 'If you want.' A very tanned woman wearing a wide silver cuff on each wrist has brought her bread in a basket and a glass of water. 'Thank you,' Claire says. 'Is she yours?' The woman laughs. 'None of these cats are anybody's, and most places don't want you to feed them. But I can't help it. Ten years and I'm still a soft touch.' Claire blinks. She ought to ask about the hotel, about Kostas, but she doesn't know how to phrase her question. 'What can I get you?' the woman asks. She orders a beer, then changes her mind, and asks for retsina instead.

★

They are on the bed, all three of them, tangled. It reminds her of play-wrestling at home with her brother. The heaviness is familiar, the warmth, the friendly struggle that shades into panic. Hot breath at her ear, unintelligible words; and then the pressure lifts, the weight lifts; it is gone, propelled away from her across the tiny room, and both of them are making sounds of disgust, swearing and spitting, as she rolls on the bed. She thinks she might be sick. She was sick before. She hears that word again, *yitharos*, and the sawing of her breath. It catches in her chest. It makes her retch. She reaches her hands out and finds the cool tiles of the floor; a clatter as she pulls herself down. The boys start laughing. Then she is staggering away towards the darkness of the bathroom, the darkest corner, away, away from whatever's going on.

★

The retsina is disgusting, sweet and cloying and vomit-sharp, but she makes herself finish the carafe, helping it down with bread, tomato salad and a plate of grilled sardines, ordered not so much for her as for the cat, which stays glued to her feet, crunching tiny bones.

As she eats, she watches the woman teach her daughter how to lay tables. First there is the white paper tablecloth, which you fold down sharply around the edges. Then there are the red napkins with the knives and forks on top. Then there are the salt and pepper shakers. And finally there is the slim vase holding the single plastic carnation. The girl, who cannot be more than ten, watches very seriously. She does her table right first time. '*Brava!*' her mother says. '*Fantastico!*'

★

There seemed to be a long silence then, a long silence in which nobody spoke. Her chin was on the toilet seat. She was sitting on her feet, which were numb. It was so silent she thought the boys had gone, and she felt strangely disappointed, as if there had been something to save of the night, as if she had wasted her chance.

But then she heard the rumble of a drawer being opened – they were looking through her clothes – and Nikos called out to her, 'Where is your friend?'

They did not want her after all. They wanted Jane. Of course of course of course.

'Sixteen,' Claire told the water in the toilet. 'Next door.'

★

Her favourite day had involved no boys at all. They got in the car and drove across the isthmus, past the port, to a stable in the arable north. Jane's parents settled themselves down in the sun and ordered wine, while a bossy young woman emerged from the farmhouse to squeeze the two girls into rubber riding boots and velvet-covered hard hats, then led them through the yard, which reeked of horse.

Claire stood, her head strangely cool inside the dome of the hat, even as the sun beat her shoulders red, and watched as the woman fetched a heavy mare for her to ride. The mare walked over to Claire with some reluctance, looked sideways at her from one huge eye, then shoved her with a flat cheek. Claire staggered back, surprised, but the woman said, 'No. Push back. She's testing.' Claire pushed on the mare's hot neck. Nothing happened. 'Good,' the woman said.

They set off at a walk down the farm track and out through the gates, and then came two hours of adjusting her rhythms to the rhythms of the horse, her rolling gait, her reluctant trot, her stopping to eat or shit, in which she forgot the usual shape of her own thoughts. She was able to brush the tops of the grasses sailing past, to see over stone walls into scrubby gardens. She was able to watch Jane on her horse in front, nervously straight-backed, bouncing in the saddle, with no feeling in the world but love.

★

'I was here when I was fifteen,' she tells the Englishwoman at the taverna. 'Me and my friend, we hung around with this boy, Kostas. Maybe you know him—'

The woman laughs. 'I know about twenty Kostases.'

Claire describes him, how old he would be now, how he used to work at the bar at Hotel Oceanis. The woman looks disbelieving. She pulls out her mobile phone. Its screen shows a man with a lopsided smile, his hairy arm thrown around the woman, and the woman's daughter, younger then, perched on his lap. 'Is that him?'

'I don't know,' Claire says, and she doesn't. It could be him. How would she tell? Who remembers the soldiers? 'It's such a long time ago,' she says. 'I'd need to ask him about it.'

The woman sighs. 'He's on the mainland. Oh, it's such a shame. I want to know now. Did you two have a thing?' She is unworried, even amused, which adds to Claire's misgivings. Kostas's daughter, if that is who she is, watches from the door of the taverna with solemn curiosity.

'My friend had a crush on him,' Claire says. 'But I don't think anything happened.'

★

They didn't do it in her room – they took her to the olive grove instead. That much Claire was allowed. Jane made her tend to the wounds on her back, bright red scratches and deeper cuts, something adult and official about it, like the proof of a ritual punishment. Claire washed them as gently as she could in the bath, then picked out the splinters with a pair of silver tweezers and applied the closest thing she could find to antiseptic, which was a cream she had brought for her spots. She helped Jane find something suitable to wear. But she couldn't persuade her to tell. '*No*,' Jane said, her whole body rigid, and Claire didn't ask her again.

★

With the taste of retsina sour in her mouth, she lies down in the dark but cannot sleep. The bed tilts. She crosses the room and puts the lamp back on. Its glow picks out the gold in the portrait of the saint. A male saint, this one, a young military man, dressed in fish-scale armour, with a red cloak tied around his collarbones. His face is small and fierce, his hair moulded curls, and he carries a thin spear across his body that points to the gold expanse of the sky. Had it been a woman, she might have considered offering some kind of a prayer.

'How was it?' asks Demetra. She has driven straight to Piraeus from work; she looks strange in her neat blue shirt. Claire shrugs, and she laughs, not unkindly. 'I told you,' she says. 'That place is a rock. Athens you will love.'

That night, back in Demetra's sister's bedroom, Claire unfolds the laptop and searches for Saint Sofia. She finds herself on Wikipedia again, but there is only a small amount of information, and little that she did not already know: a date, a town, a prayer.

Thou didst blossom in the courts of the Lord as a fruitful olive tree, O holy Martyr Sophia; in thy contest thou didst offer to Christ the sweet fruit of thy womb, Love, Hope and Faith. With them intercede for us all.

*

They flew home in silence, Jane's parents exchanging glances of amusement at their daughter's excess. They knew she had been drinking the night before. That was all they knew. Back in England, Claire accompanied Jane to the clinic to obtain the necessary pill. She read dog-eared magazines in the waiting room, until Jane emerged, red with indignation. 'Condescending bitch.'

'Was she awful? What did she say?'

'Come on, before we see someone.'

'Do we need to go to Boots?'

'I've got it.' She clutched the foil packet in her hand. 'Let's get a Coke and get this over with.'

They went to McDonald's. They shredded the wrappers from their straws. Then Jane said she felt funny, she was going home.

Each time they went to town that summer, Jane brought a new friend, then another, girls who smudged their eyes and smoked. Claire began to hear about excursions after they happened: a trip to the cinema, to the indoor shopping centre. When school started, Jane had bobbed her hair. The new friends pretended Claire didn't exist; they surrounded Jane, shielded her. When Claire approached her in the queue for lunch one day, Jane said, 'God, Claire, what do you *want*?'

Claire flinched, but did not retreat.

'Stop – following me – around. You're like *feeding* on my life.'

'I'm worried about you.'

'She's worried about me?' Jane laughed. 'She doesn't even know what happened!' The friends laughed too. Did *they*? Claire couldn't tell. She was desperate to have this conversation alone, to draw Jane back, but everyone was listening now.

'She thinks I didn't like it,' Jane said. 'She can't imagine a girl that would.'

★

She forgets herself in Athens, where she and Demetra have three days together, endless thick coffee in small white cups, hours of walking, wine late at night; she forgets herself until the final afternoon, when they try to enter a catacomb but find the studded doors are shut. 'Siesta,' Demetra says.

Outside the doors, in a sunken courtyard, two trees burst silently from the flagstones, their boles painted white. Beneath the trees are altars, shallow brass basins full of water and shale, in which several tall thin earwax-coloured candles are burning. One basin is waist-high, the other level with Claire's chest. This one, Demetra says, is for devotions to the dead, and this one, the higher, for the saints.

Claire drops her silver bracelet through the slot, hears it splash down into a pool of devotional coins, and draws her own candle from the rack. She pauses. Nobody died and nobody is a saint. It is not clear what she ought to do – what she is trying to do. She has touched her candle to the flame of another. Now she holds the long slim shaft of it lightly, balanced like a spear across her palm.

WOULD YOU RATHER

Even after I'd chopped my hair off, a gesture of aggressive self-fashioning to make me look more punk, more like Lori Petty in *Tank Girl*, people would ask me to babysit. Maybe they saw my ugly crop, the sweatband of acne it left exposed, and thought I was a safer bet than a pretty girl.

My easiest job was the Fishers. Mr Fisher was a colleague of my father's. The kids were just babies, fast asleep before I arrived. The monitor on the coffee table never made a peep, so I'd watch TV, or read the smutty book I'd found hidden among the John Grishams on their shelves. Afterwards, Mr Fisher dropped me home. In the car with him and his musky, heady aftershave – nothing like my father's Old Spice – I'd imagine him making a pass at me. He never did.

'Where did they go?' my mother would be waiting to ask me. 'Were they drunk when they came back?'

'I don't know,' I'd say, truthfully. Were they drunk or just happy? How could you tell?

Once, Mrs Fisher asked after my brother, Liam. This was when he'd been suspended from school. One of the sixth-formers had seen him throwing stones into a tree. She'd gone closer, expecting to see a ball stuck up there, or maybe a squirrel, but it had been a Year 7 with his head cut open. It turned out Liam had been picking on him for months.

'What a difficult time,' Mrs Fisher had said. 'Your poor mother. Give her our best.'

'And what did you say to that?' my mother asked.

I told her I'd said thank you.

'Christ Almighty. You need to learn when you're being insulted.'

This was something I'd heard her say before, to my father, after they'd had people round. She often sniped at him like this. She wanted him to hold forth like her friends' husbands did, droning on over dry-roasted peanuts about restructuring, and she'd question him brightly, especially in front of others, hoping he would relent. He wouldn't. He was obstinate too, in his way. 'Nobody wants to hear shop-talk,' he'd say. At the time I took this for mordancy – people liked him for it – but now it seems more like despair. Things were not going well for him at work. Eventually I came home from school and found him on the sofa, still in his dressing gown and pyjamas. He'd been sidelined, my mother explained. Mr Fisher and Co. had squeezed him out. My father hung around the place in his dressing gown for months, like a smelly ghost. I didn't sit for the Fishers again.

During the time when I was earning no extra money, I filled two pages of my notebook with a want-list of CDs:

Offspring, Green Day, poppy punk for teens who weren't even born when the real thing died. I considered myself rebellious, though not enough to steal what I couldn't afford. My father stayed in the computer room with the curtains closed. Liam stayed in his bedroom. Only my mother busied around, tidying and washing dishes and sighing and turning the television up and down. And then one day, at the garden centre, she bumped into Dr Harmer from down the road, and he complained how difficult it was to find a reliable girl to look after Elizabeth: he needed someone on Thursday nights, when he and his wife went to amateur dramatics at the Methodist church. My mother suggested me. I was very independent. I'd done it before. Dr Harmer would pay ten pounds. Hadn't she done the right thing? When I just shrugged and went on crunching crisps, she said, 'For God's sake! It's bad enough your Dad moping around all day. Can't you do something useful?'

The Harmers' was a Victorian house with a shabby, lopsided look. The lawn was boggy, the swing half-sunk, the bed of black poppies almost always in the shade. They'd have bought it for the hedges, the detachment, the good state school on the hill, but prioritising these qualities, ignoring the gloomy aspect and unmanageable size, meant that the house would get the better of them. It was that kind of area, where either the house or the occupant won.

Dr Harmer let me in, muttering that they'd be out of my hair in a minute, as if I'd come to fumigate the place. He was a GP at a surgery on the other side of the ring road. I found him aloof and neglectful of material things, just as I thought a doctor ought to be, and old – much older than my father. Mrs Harmer was Australian. An Australian, on our road! I couldn't understand why she'd choose to live *here*, away from all the surfing and the sharks. Personally I intended to move to America as soon as I could.

She showed me the emergency phone number pinned to the corkboard. She said, 'Now this is very important: make sure Elizabeth takes one of these before she goes to bed,' holding out a packet of tablets. The printed foil said *Warfarin Sodium 0.5 mg*. 'We'll be back by ten. She can have a hot chocolate if she wants.' She called up the stairs, 'Elizabeth? The sitter's here. We're going now' – though she pronounced it *goyng*. Then she stood for a moment, wringing her big dry hands. It was nothing like the Fishers' exits, all dressed up and eager to go.

The Harmers didn't have any interesting books on their shelves. The rooms were huge, but they hadn't got enough furniture in them, leaving great hairy expanses of carpet to cross on which you could get miserably stranded like a spider. At the top of the staircase was a grandfather clock and a door standing ajar against peach-painted walls.

'Oh *good*,' Elizabeth cried, whirling to greet me, leaping off her bed, 'you're here!'

Her voice had a strange twang, a staginess, like when English children play at accents they've only heard on TV. 'Look at this,' she said, and lifted up her top.

A pink and white scar ran from the dip in her collarbone down to where her ribs butterflied away from each other.

The scar tissue was raised, like a welt, and shiny, like a burn, but the wound had obviously been surgical: it was neat and straight, and I could see little spokes coming off it where the stitches had healed.

'I had three operations,' she said. 'I had a splashy valve. They had to go in and look around, and then they had to fix it, and then that didn't work, so they had to go in again.'

'Put your top down,' I said. There was another scar, older, whiter, curving around under – what to call it? Where her left breast was going to be. 'You don't just show that to people. It's private. It's your private parts.'

She let the top fall, as if her revelation hadn't happened, and went on to something else, some tale about how Scarlet had painted an extra numeral on the clock face between nine and ten, and when it chimed we'd be imprisoned for ever in a make-believe hour, never getting any older than we were, and her parents would never return.

'Who's Scarlet?'

'She's a spy – sort of a spy. She's a girl. She doesn't follow any rules and she's very, very dangerous. She kidnapped Mary-Bell, and we have to get her back, but we *have* to go in disguise ...'

She was radiant, imperious, revolting. Her breath smelled like sausages – dinner, or tonsillitis? Was she feverish? Was she ill? She started pulling old hats and coats from a basket and thrusting them towards me. My mother had told me Dr Harmer had a son, much older, from his first marriage, but that the son lived in Vancouver now and never came to visit, so Elizabeth was basically an only child. Feeling sorry for her, I took a hat, a floppy velvet thing, and put it on.

My favourite babysitter had been a girl called Nerys, with beautifully clear skin — she'd let me touch her cheek sometimes, so moist it was tacky — and a brusque, dismissive manner that was not unkind. Nerys would never join in with games. She stayed on the sofa, drinking cherry Coke, reading fashion magazines with the TV on. Sometimes she talked a bit about boys, or clubs, amused I'd asked. Her thudding answers were not interesting in themselves but because they seemed absolutely truthful. Yes, she had boyfriends. Yes, she went out. Yes, she drank, but it wasn't that nice.

She fell out, once, spectacularly, with her mother. She left home, and only kept sitting for me because she needed the money. My mother kept booking her so she could ring up Nerys's mother afterwards and tell her how Nerys was doing. I'd confessed this once to Nerys: that my mother was spying on her, reporting on her. I thought she'd be shocked, but she wasn't. She told me to mind my own business. I didn't get to touch her cheek that night. Then she went away to university, and my mother and Nerys's mother lost touch. Most of my mother's friends were like that: people with whom she had some structural reason to stay in contact, who drifted at the structure's end.

I wiped condensation off Elizabeth's bedroom window. She had a crow's-eye-view of the lawn and hedges, the cul-de-sac, the neighbours' gardens lit by security lights. Uphill, out of sight, was my own house. Past it lay the woods, the field,

the school. Dominic was out there somewhere. Dominic was
a boy I fancied. He sat behind me in History and kicked
the back of my chair. His blonde forearms in my peripheral
vision were a torment. Once I'd overheard him saying loudly,
triumphantly, 'Mate – I came like a fucking *fountain*', and felt
a flame roar up in my chest. He lived on the other side of
the valley. I knew he had friends from other schools. I knew
he smoked. What else did I know? He wouldn't stay on for
sixth form. Once he'd said he wanted to be a tattoo artist.
His copies from H. R. Giger, very beautiful and steady, were
pinned to the wall in the art room. And once he'd talked
about metalwork. He meant belt buckles, bracelets, things
like that, but still I pictured him labouring, like a blacksmith,
in a forge.

Our interactions were abrupt and entirely on his terms. He
would throw a biro at the back of my head, and when I turned
around he would say, 'There's a helicopter crash. Everybody
dies except you. But you've got to lose something. What is
it – your hands, or your feet?' There was a rage at school for
concocting dilemmas that forced the listener to choose one
terrible option over another: drink some piss or eat a spider,
fuck a pig or fuck a cow, always smell of cheese or never earn
much money. You had to choose quickly, as if the answer
was obvious, and once your decision was made it had to be
defended at all costs. Usually that was the end of it, but then
Dominic pushed me under the stairs outside Biology and
asked me what I was doing that night, the night I was due
at the Harmers'. I'd told him I had to babysit. He'd told me
he'd be there at eight o'clock.

We were playing when the doorbell rang. Elizabeth leapt from vacant dreaminess to vindication. '*Scarlet!* It's *her!*'

I tore the hat off my head. 'Stay here.'

The door opened on one blue eye, half a black sweatshirt and a dirty green Van. 'You've got some freaky black flowers out here.'

'You mean the poppies?'

'Are they poppies?'

He vanished.

'Hello?' I put my head outside and listened, but all I heard was a cat's childish noise. With one sentence I'd sent him shooting back where he'd come from. I hadn't known it was possible to disappoint a person so quickly. Now I'd tell Elizabeth that Scarlet was gone, mix her a hot chocolate, and watch *The X-Files*. It didn't seem so terrible a prospect. But then Dominic called my name.

Elizabeth crouched on the stairs. 'Don't go! That's what she wants!'

'Shut the door,' I said.

He was kneeling in the flower bed. He'd picked some poppies already: they flopped against his wrist. I actually thought he was picking them for me. Half to himself, he said, 'How many d'you think we need?' When I didn't answer, he lurched towards the house.

Elizabeth had put the chain on. She demanded to know who Dominic was, why he'd picked their flowers.

'They're for tea,' I said. 'Tea that Scarlet can't drink. He's a spy too. He's come to get her.'

Elizabeth stared. 'Are you a spy?'

'Oh, yes,' he said, with an irony that was painful to me. 'I'm a massive spy. With a little eye.'

When she let us in, he went straight to the kitchen. He put the kettle on. He got a knife and a chopping board and started smashing the poppyheads flat with the blade, like cloves of garlic.

'They're not those kind of poppies,' I said. 'Opium poppies are illegal.'

'Can't be that different, can they? Same family.'

He pushed the mess into a glass teapot and poured in boiling water. It turned a purplish grey. He put some in a cup, drank it, gave a big bark of a cough, and spat into the sink.

'That's disgusting,' Elizabeth said.

Dominic stuck out his bruising tongue. 'Old Scarlet,' he said. 'What a bitch. She was hiding in the trees outside.' Off Elizabeth ran, in that funny way she had, high up on the balls of her feet. 'This is fucking shit,' he said to me. 'Have they got any booze?'

I felt afraid, then. Poppies could be explained as a potion, part of Elizabeth's games, but alcohol was a power I didn't want to summon. I watched him go to the cellar head and touch the ranks of bottles.

'Don't,' I said. 'They'll know.'

'They won't.' He lifted out a bottle of whisky. 'I'll top it up.' He grinned.

'Don't take too much,' I said, adding a lame, 'please.'

Every drop he poured seemed to come from my vein. The cup was half-full before he stopped. He topped the bottle up with water and replaced it as Elizabeth returned.

'Scarlet's not there,' she complained. 'We should search the house.'

This was the last thing I wanted, but Dominic said it was a great idea, and lurched off, cup in hand. Elizabeth scampered after him. We looked in the bathroom, the spare room, Elizabeth's bedroom, an empty room that was maybe once the son's. Dominic clunked his cup against the last closed door. 'What about here?'

'That's my parents' room. We don't play in there.'

'Perfect. That's exactly where she'll be.'

Elizabeth looked at me in alarm. I shrugged. 'I thought she didn't follow any rules?'

I followed Dominic into the bedroom. 'Watch out,' he said. He stepped behind the door, thrust it shut, and turned the key in the lock.

'What happened?' Elizabeth wailed. 'What happened?'

Dominic called, 'Scarlet locked us in!' Then he went straight to the nightstand and began to open the drawers.

The Harmers' bedroom was where all their furniture was hiding. A chest of drawers and a dressing table stood jammed together under the window, their surfaces alive with candles, ornaments, toiletries and pots of dead – or paper? – flowers. An ancient TV-VCR faced the bed. Layers of rugs covered the floor, piles of dirty clothes in heaps, a metal ironing board with a rusted iron perched on it, pictureless frames leaning against the skirting boards. Elizabeth was still yelling outside, something about fixing the clock, but the shut door and masses of stuff muffled her voice.

'Holy shit.' Dominic was holding up a videotape. 'This is some old porn. 1970s. Look at that hair.'

The chunky case, orange and pink, showed a woman on the front with her arms flung open. *Deep Throat*, it said, a phrase I associated only with *The X-Files*. He put the tape in the VCR, and a scene leapt up, all combed with wavy lines: a man, wearing a yellow shirt, going down on a woman. The man's fluffy sideburns were like the fluffy reddish hair on the woman's labia. One of her hands cradled his head, her beige nails gleaming. There was a strange cheery song playing, and a noise in the background like someone blowing through a straw into their Coke. Somehow we were both sitting on the Harmers' bed. When Dominic mashed his mouth against mine, I wondered who he was kissing. Did it matter? The kiss was happening, I told myself. It was happening and I was inside it. I pulled away.

'What's wrong?'

'Nothing. It's just . . . She's gone quiet. I'm supposed to be looking after her.'

He was so close I could see the spoke of green in the blue wheel of his iris, the tight creamy pinprick of pus in the head of a spot.

'D'you wanna go out with me,' he murmured, 'or what?' His hand was on my thigh, burning through my jeans.

'She could be anywhere.' I looked down. 'She's not normal.' I got up and stopped the tape. 'She's got a heart condition.'

Elizabeth wasn't on the landing. She wasn't in her room. I came back in time to see Dominic eject the tape from the

VCR and tuck it inside his sweatshirt; then he thundered down the stairs and left the house. We never spoke again.

Elizabeth was sitting at the kitchen table.

'Time for bed,' I told her.

'No it's not.'

'Have you taken your tablet?'

'I never go this early.'

'You're going when I say you are.'

I dragged her chair out while she was still sitting on it, and she leapt like a cat. For a second I knew I'd got away with something. Then she said, 'Stop it, I'm waiting for Scarlet,' and I was furious all over again.

'Scarlet's not real.'

'She is!'

'You made her up, I played along, and now it's time for bed.'

I had the weirdest feeling then that Scarlet was in the room after all. She'd come into being the moment I'd denied her, standing behind me, in Elizabeth's line of sight, pulling a horrible face at my back. If I turned quickly enough, I would see her.

'If you want to play a game,' I said, 'let's play something less babyish.'

'Like what?'

'I give you two choices, and you have to pick one.'

'All right,' Elizabeth said, too quickly. She thought I was giving her a choice of two games.

'Your parents have been kidnapped. The ransom's a million pounds each, but you've only got one million and you can't get any more. Who are you going to save?'

She glared at me. 'They *haven't* been kidnapped.'

'It's a game. You've got to imagine.'

'You can't make me imagine that.'

Maybe she wasn't so weird after all, because she found the dilemma intolerable. Her eyes filled with tears.

'You can't *ask* me that,' she repeated, but the stubbornness was gone.

'Fine,' I said. 'Stick to your imaginary friends. And go to sleep. I've got homework to do.'

'Wait,' she said, reaching for me. Her fingers were cold. 'I really can't get more money? What if I sold the house?'

'You've sold the house. Time's nearly up.'

'What if I won't choose?'

I rolled my eyes. 'What do you *think*?'

I could've risen above myself, told her to forget it, made her a cup of hot chocolate after all, but even when the tears started running down her face I waited for an answer.

'My Dad,' she whispered. 'I'd save my Dad.'

Her choice hung between us, savagely, innocently beautiful, like an icicle. I said, 'If you tell anyone Dominic was here, I'll tell your mother what you just told me.'

I scrubbed the purple stains on the chopping board for a long time, until I realised it didn't matter. Dominic's theft would become my theft. Any extra failings would not be reckoned up. I left the board in the sink and went upstairs. Elizabeth's night-light threw a reddish glow under the door, and I envied her sorrowful sleep. In the morning it would all be washed away, the clock would reset, Scarlet would return, and they'd start the game again. Not for me. I'd have to go to school, and there would be Dominic, knowing what he knew.

I went into the Harmers' room and looked in the drawer. It was full of labelled VHS tapes, the kind my mother used to record *Love Hurts*. The labels were handwritten in biro: 8/7/89, 12/5/91 ... I chose one at random, fed it into the machine, and pressed play.

It was a hotel room. Light streamed through net curtains. A woman lounged on the bed with her back to the handheld camera. The cameraman said something, a deep mumble I couldn't make out, and she turned towards him, smiling under a heavy fringe. There was less grey in her hair, and the fringe was gone now, but I recognised Mrs Harmer straight away. The cameraman – surely Dr Harmer – reached out and touched her cheek, then dropped his hand and tugged open the dressing gown she was wearing. She was naked underneath, and pregnant. I stared at the beige drum of her belly, the swollen breasts lolling on top. She rolled on to her side, and the camera hovered over her, turning to catch the cameraman's naked thigh entering the frame, then his cock, bright pink and jutting. They started moving together, gentle motions, as if the bed were a boat lifting on the swell. At a certain point, Dr Harmer put the camera down on the bedspread, pointing back at his wife, so the screen filled up with her shining curves, and every so often his curly head appeared beyond her shoulder, as if he was running behind her, trying to keep up.

I pushed my hand down my jeans and concentrated on myself. The room shrank. My body swelled to fill it. My hand cramped. I was pressed upon, contained. The pressure built. Dominic's kiss was in my mind when the spasms ran through me, *Dominic*, even the name, a word I spoke out loud to myself, but late, missing the moment. I opened my eyes, and was vaguely shocked to see them still going at it, then confused by a glimpse over Dr Harmer's heaving shoulder of a third figure looming behind them, a girl with red hair and a long, pale, mischievous face, holding – of all things – a magnifying glass.

'What're you doing?'

It was Elizabeth. I leapt forward and smashed the STOP button with my sticky fist. The scene wobbled and froze, but didn't disappear, although the girl was gone, eclipsed again by Dr Harmer's shoulder. I wheeled around angrily. 'You don't sneak up like that!'

Her hands were pressed to her belly, which still protruded like a younger child's. 'I feel poorly,' she complained.

'You shouldn't be out of bed. Go back to your room. I'll be there in a minute.'

'What are you watching?' She was looking at the screen, at her mother's breasts, anonymous but clearly exposed.

'Nothing. None of your business.'

She belched – a belch that had a retch folded up in the end of it. 'I think I'm going to be sick.'

'You can't be sick *here*. You need to go the bathroom.'

But there wasn't time. She dropped and puked with unnatural force. Dark liquid dripped off her chin and soaked the carpet. She was shivering all over, pale and slightly sweaty. Her nightie was thin and white and printed with faded hearts, and the ridge of her spine showed through the fabric when the retching arched her back. I went to her, and put my hand on her shoulder. The fabric was clinging to her skin, a fearsome heat powering through it. Little chunks of half-digested mush sat on top of the carpet's pile, and a white pip that could have been what was left of her Warfarin tablet.

'You silly girl,' I said. 'What did you do?' But I already knew. She'd drunk the tea Dominic had made. I'd poisoned her and she was going to die.

A line of spit slid from her lip to the floor. We heard the key turn in the lock downstairs, and then the grandfather clock on the landing struck the hour and started to chime. It must be ten, I thought. They'd said they'd be back by ten. Whatever control Elizabeth had been maintaining finally dissolved, and she wailed for her mother.

'Don't shout!' I hissed. 'Go down! Go down and see her!'

But now she was really crying, breaking off her sobs of 'Mum!' to retch again.

Mrs Harmer called back, faintly, 'Elizabeth? Are you all right?'

I couldn't just leave the tape in the machine for them to find. There were Mrs Harmer's dark nipples filling the screen. I needed to get Elizabeth out of the room, on to the landing. I needed to stay beside her. If only there had been two of me! If only I'd had my own Scarlet, sprung from my brain! But the Harmers were in the hall by now, throwing off their coats. They were calling for their daughter, they were climbing the stairs, it was almost the worst of all possible worlds. The clock chimed ten and kept going. Elizabeth wailed for her mother, then stopped to retch, but nothing came up. A line of spit slid from her lip to the floor.

'Elizabeth?' Mrs Harmer called faintly. 'Are you all right?'

Of course she wasn't. She'd drunk the tea Dominic had made. I'd poisoned her and she was going to die.

'You silly girl,' I said. 'What did you do?'

MUSTER'S PUPPETS PRESENTS . . .

Claire was coming over with her boyfriend – her *partner* –
and Joan was baking mince pies in preparation, though she
couldn't remember whether Claire liked mince pies. It was
difficult to keep everything straight with four children who
changed their preferences every week, so she'd put straw-
berry jam in some of them instead, because who doesn't
like jam?

They'd had nothing for six months, then Claire phoned
the landline, out of the blue, and asked if they'd be at
home tomorrow, so she could come round. The week
before Christmas. They'd steeled themselves not to hear
from her at all, which was exactly what had happened
two Christmases ago, the voicemails unresponded-to, the
texts unanswered: a bewildering, unnatural silence that
had settled over Joan's head like one of those hoods you
put on falcons, and lasted far into the new year, and was
never explained.

Henry came in. 'That's the light working now. Not that she's going to notice.'

'It isn't for her,' Joan said. 'It's for us.'

Joan and Henry ran a B&B from a house they couldn't afford, a sprawling seven-bedroomed place on the edge of a town once famous for its salty hard cheese and its Sunday market. Three of its rooms were let out every night, usually to travelling businessmen, small-timers who still used a Filofax, whose client base was dying off, and also to older couples on modest holidays, walkers, people Joan needn't worry about; though occasionally a younger pair came through, professional, sometimes southern, in town for a friend's wedding. These younger couples looked impossibly clean and arrogant to Joan. They breezed in and out with matching smirks on their faces; they appreciated the John Lewis salt and pepper grinders at breakfast, the Farrow & Ball paint on the stairs, but she could see them thinking that they'd never end up like this, serving strangers in their own home, running down the clock. They were expecting to live lives in which the end is never in sight until it's upon you.

Claire had loved these guests when she was little. She'd make a nuisance of herself, bothering the girls about their jewellery, until Joan would have to send her out of the breakfast room on some mission or other. When she'd gone, the couples would look knowingly at one another across their poached eggs, basking in Claire's admiration for them, flirting with the idea of themselves as mothers and fathers, ones who'd do anything to make their child feel loved. Just you wait, Joan had thought, skimming off the poaching water. Just you wait till you're settled and the girl's your own.

She'd got one of those couples staying at the moment. Two nights. She didn't think it was a wedding. They had arrived yesterday, after eight o'clock and smelling of wine, though they'd driven up in the boyfriend's car. He was very upright and very slim, with a permanent smile, as if to say, *My life's wonderful, isn't yours?* The girl was one of those executive types: even here, on a Sunday morning, she'd come down dressed as if she might've been going to a business meeting. Maybe she was. But these days there was nobody around to admire her silver tennis bracelet, her polished bag. Tessa, Joan's youngest, was seventeen, so shy she avoided the breakfast room at all costs, and – as it happened – still asleep, though it was nearly midday.

Henry was tidying the living room: she could hear him pummelling cushions. Richard, back from university for the holidays, had gone out already for a bike ride, and the eldest, Neal, wouldn't be home for another two days, if he made it at all. Joan allowed herself to believe that he would; she allowed herself to imagine all six of them under the same roof for Christmas that year, and rolled her pastry a fraction thinner. Richard would come back muddy and hungry from his ride, he'd stuff the pies without thinking into his mouth, and she couldn't begrudge him that. She sealed them with egg wash and put them in the oven, and then she heard tyres on the gravel outside.

'Henry?'

'It's just Room Two,' he called.

That was the couple, back already. They'd only been gone three hours. It was something the younger ones did, coming and going through the day, as if it was a hotel. They disappeared up to their rooms, and there might be noises. Joan was not an idiot. She knew people had sex in her house: she was the one who stripped the bedclothes and put them in the wash. It was not a pleasant fact, but it was part of the business she'd chosen to run. It seemed unnecessary, though, for guests to do it in the daytime, then lounge in bed when Joan was up and working. It suggested that they thought of her as a cleaner, an invisible member of their hospitality staff, rather than – as she considered herself – a landlady or proprietress.

'Tessie?' She knocked hard on Tessa's door, then pushed inside. Sleepy stillness greeted her, a stale smell, and something rumbling away on the laptop, rain and thunder, because Tessie claimed she couldn't sleep without background noise. 'Tessie, get up. Your sister's coming round.'

Normally Tessa would lie and doze, but today she sat up quickly, as if she'd been pulled on a string. 'Claire's coming?'

'What other sister have you got?'

Joan gathered dirty mugs from the shelves and took them back down with her. Science experiments, Henry called them. They were part of the stale smell, the green powders they contained; but not the whole of it. Tessa's was not a clean shyness. There was something furtive and greasy in it, something Joan didn't want to know.

Claire was twenty-five; the man standing beside her was clearly past forty. 'Mark,' he said, putting out his hand, and

Joan recoiled. He looked heavy – not fat, but muscular, broad-shouldered, large-boned, with an oddly narrow, fluted nose. And was that a tattoo snaking down his wrist? Claire appeared delicate beside him, though she wasn't. She stood in the middle of the kitchen as though it wasn't hers, as though she'd never seen the place before. It was Mark who looked at ease: a studied kind of looseness, challenging somehow.

'You've changed the cupboards,' Claire said. Her voice had an accusatory note that Joan immediately remembered.

'Would you like to sit down?'

'We've been scrunched in the car for an hour.'

Joan stopped herself asking where they'd driven from, why it had taken an hour. Last she knew, Claire had been living in a shared house in Radcliffe, but that was ten months ago. It all could've changed.

'So, Mark,' Henry ventured, 'what is it you do?'

Mark nodded, without surprise, as if he'd been waiting for this question. 'I coach people, Henry,' he said.

'Rugby? Boxing?'

'I'm a life coach, actually. So a little bit of fitness, yeah, but it's more than that.'

Joan could tell that Henry didn't know what life coaching was. Joan did. She'd thought about trying it herself, and now she was glad she never had. She asked, 'Is that how you met?'

'I'm not paying him,' Claire said, instantly, 'if that's what you mean.'

'It was a meet-up,' Mark said, and now it was Joan's turn to be confused. He could see it, and began to smile. He explained that he did a lot of stuff online. People watched, they commented and joined in. He coached online, too. (That made sense. Claire had spent thousands of hours online when she'd lived at home. They'd had to switch the hub off to get her to bed.) Sometimes he did a random meet-up somewhere, getting face-to-face with the fans. He appeared to say 'fans' without irony. Perhaps Joan wasn't attuned to his tone yet. Or perhaps he was actually famous, what passed for famous these days. Claire came along to one of the meet-ups, Mark continued. They hit it off straight away. They went for a drink, didn't they? The rest is history, he said, though it was news to Joan, and delivered too easily, too directly, without any of the nerves you'd expect from a boyfriend meeting the parents for the first time. That was his age, she supposed. He might be closer to Henry's than he was to Claire's.

'And you enjoy it,' Henry asked, 'this coaching?'

'People transforming their lives? What could be better than that?' Mark's spread hands were casual, but his tone was unappealingly serious. Not that different from Claire's other boyfriends, then. She'd always gone for men who couldn't laugh at themselves.

'It's all about transformations these days, isn't it?' Joan said. 'Makeovers and things. Getting rid of all your posses-sions. Moving to Australia. Maybe that's what we need to do. Maybe we need to sell up and move to Australia.'

Claire's mouth twitched, as if to say, *maybe you do*. Or was Joan imagining that? Normally she could tell when someone was being funny with her. The kids had made a joke of it years ago, how Mum always thought you were being funny with her, or the woman in the shop was, or so-and-so's friend. But with Claire she had not been able to decide. When would they finally be old enough to *see* them at last – to see what you'd made – to know them as strangers and think to yourself, yes, we've things in common, or no, we've nothing at all? When would she know if she *liked* her daughter?

Henry was asking everyone and no one if they wanted coffee.

'No. Actually.' Claire paused, and Mark touched her arm. It seemed like a supportive gesture, though later Joan would wonder. 'I'd like to clear my old stuff out of my room. Have you got some bin bags, please?'

Claire's old room was Tessa's room now. They had shared when they were little, then Tessa had moved down to Neal's room when Neal left. When Claire left too, Tessa had wanted to move back, so they'd put all Claire's stuff into the cupboard: the room had a deep cupboard that went right back into the eaves. Claire had made a den of this for her and Tess when they were younger. She'd run fairy lights into it and put blankets on the floor. It was an eighth room, really, if you didn't mind crouching all the time. She'd even put a sign on the door, Room Eight, in wobbly script. Occasionally, she'd slept in there all night, careless of the silverfish, the cold.

Claire and Mark spent hours going through the cupboard. Claire stayed upstairs the whole time, sorting through her stuff, while Mark carried the bin bags down and loaded them into his car.

'We can take those,' Joan said, and Henry agreed: he said, 'You can leave the rubbish,' but Mark politely insisted that they would be driving past the tip either way. He had already carried a couple of transparent crates upstairs, which Claire would presumably fill with things she wanted to keep, if she wanted to keep anything at all. Joan watched the procession of black bin bags, the rising pile in the car's dropped backseat, and despaired. How could she want so little? Disposing of the Barbies and the ancient birthday cards was one thing, but what about her notes from university, her artwork from GCSE?

Joan remembered the struggle to decide what to keep from her own mother's house. The glass bead necklaces, heavy, like strings of marbles. The ugly squadron of Toby jugs. But that had been unavoidable. Her mother had been dead, a stroke at seventy-six – would Claire even remember? – and Joan's brothers were worse than useless at practical things, so she'd left Henry with the kids and done it herself in one weekend. And those had been her mother's things, not Joan's. She wondered for a moment where her own schoolbooks were, and found that she didn't know. She and Henry had a deep cupboard in their room, too, full of old suitcases, and curtains too short for this house's windows, and the boxed-up Toby jugs. Perhaps she would look for them later.

Mark dumped another bag in the car. When he'd powered back upstairs, Joan ventured out across the gravel and looked into the open boot. The bags lay slumped heavily across one another. Their twisted ends wrinkled and breathed. One was untied: she plunged her hand in, a lucky dip, grabbed the spine of something, and pulled it out. She'd been hoping for a schoolbook – something full of Claire's sweet round handwriting from before she forcibly changed it, age fourteen, to a

spiky mess – but it was a programme: *Muster's Puppets presents
. . . A Journey Round the Moon.*

She was amazed. Claire had always maintained that she
could not remember going to see this show at the church
hall, though Joan had taken her twice, she loved it so much.
This had been before Tessa, when Richard was tiny and Neal
was away at school. She'd taken Richard in his pushchair,
and miraculously he'd slept through the whole thing, both
times, while Claire had crept forward through the chairs and
sat on the dusty floor at the front with other children, with
strangers. She hadn't been frightened of the puppets at all,
though they were enormous, with marrow-sized heads that
broke in half when they talked, that were operated by the men
and women dressed all in black, with black balaclavas. When
they got home, Claire had tried to make a puppet of her own,
with pink felt and polystyrene and a dowel rod; she'd called it
'Suzanne', and worn her black cagoule with the hood up and
carried it around the house. Suzanne had talked in a strangled
voice, high in the back of Claire's throat; it passed comment
on what everyone was doing, though its mouth wouldn't open
and close. God, that puppet! Joan had hated it, hated the weird
insistence with which Claire reached for it every morning,
how she greeted the postman with it – and when she'd brought
it into the breakfast room, where the B&B guests were eating,
and made it go from table to table interviewing them about
their plans for the day, Joan had marched Claire out of there,
Suzanne protesting in its strangled voice, while the guests
laughed nervously into their coffee and thought that perhaps
they would not stay at Joan's on their next excursion.

She'd taken Suzanne away, in fact. She'd put it in a black bin bag in the cupboard in her and Henry's room, and told Claire that she couldn't have it back for a month – and when the month had passed, Claire hadn't mentioned it, and neither had Joan.

At last Claire emerged, smudged and tired, and accepted some tea, though not a jam tart. Mark wanted pints of water. They sat at the kitchen table, and after a long silence, Claire said, 'I'm not happy,' as if she had expected to be.

'No,' Henry murmured.

'I feel like I've felt this way for a long time.'

Joan said, 'This is the first I'm hearing about it.'

'It's not. I've tried to tell you.'

'When have you tried?'

'Lots of times.'

'But when?'

'Claire,' Henry said, 'you can always talk to us. You know that.'

'I think what Claire's saying' – this was Mark – 'is that she talks, but she isn't sure you listen.'

'Of course we listen,' Joan said. 'When have we not listened?'

'I've asked you not to keep forwarding me job adverts,' Claire said.

Claire had been temping at the same accountancy firm since she'd finished her degree. It wasn't temping any more, it was a proper secretarial job, just without any of the benefits. She typed up letters, she answered the phone, but it wasn't what she wanted to do with her life. It couldn't be. So Joan

MUSTER'S PUPPETS PRESENTS ...

sent her adverts for graduate jobs from time to time: where
was the harm in that?

'I hardly ever send them,' she said.

'I don't want you to send them *at all*. I've told you that. I
said it three years ago. Why's it so hard?'

'So just ignore them. Delete them as soon as they arrive.'

'I don't want to have to see them!'

'Well.' Joan sat back in her chair. 'You've got a lot to say for
yourself today. It's not so long ago you wouldn't say anything
at all. Does he know about *that*?'

'He knows everything. He knows me better than you.'

'It was half a year, Claire. Half a year when you lived in
this house and you wouldn't say a word. That was very difficult for us.'

'But she's over it now, aren't you?' Henry said.

'No, Dad, that's what I'm saying. I'm unhappy. I'm
depressed.'

Joan resented instantly the formal foreclosure of the word,
its clinical power. 'I'm sorry to hear that,' she said. 'I know
things haven't been easy for you recently.'

'It's not just recently. It's been years.'

'Well, I'm sorry to hear that,' Joan said again. 'But depression's a chemical thing, you know, it's a chemical imbalance.
That's why antidepressants are so effective.'

'Depression,' Claire said, her voice wavering, 'is withheld
knowledge.'

'Oh Claire. You don't even sound like yourself. Where
did you get that from?'

'It's John Layard,' Mark said.

'What's that?'

'A Jungian analyst; a very good one, actually.'

'I'm telling you,' Claire said. 'My depression comes from feeling things and knowing things that I'm not allowed to express.'

'Like what?' Joan asked. 'Not allowed by who? By me?' Claire didn't answer. 'Don't be silly,' Joan said. 'You can tell me' – she stopped short of saying *anything* – 'whatever you want.'

'I can tell you what you want to hear.'

'That's not true. You've just told me you're depressed. That's not something I wanted to hear.'

'Isn't it?'

'Of course it's not!'

Claire was crying now, though it didn't stop her from talking. Her accusations became confused: that Joan had never paid attention to her, that Henry just let Joan do everything her way, that they had never taught Claire how to look after herself, that they had allowed her to see one of her teachers when she was still at school. It was amazing to Joan that she could say this with the boyfriend sitting right beside her. But Mark didn't blink. He said, 'Claire and I have ended up together because that's how her sexuality was formed. She engaged with an older man at a very formative point in her life.'

Her sexuality! Joan nearly laughed. I cleaned up your shit, she wanted to tell her. I cleaned up your shit and your piss and your vomit, I combed the nits out of your hair, I put calamine lotion on your chickenpox blisters, and did I mention the shit?

Did I mention the times you shit the bed even though you were basically too old to do something like that, and I had to come in and gather the sheets up around it, this hot stinking little parcel, gather it up and flip it into the toilet, soak the sheets in bleach, put the washer on at three in the morning? How many other people's bodily fluids have *you* had to deal with in your life? None. Your cat's, maybe. You scoop hard matted cat shit out of a litter box with a plastic spade and you think you understand what it is to be a caregiver.

'We're not here to lay blame,' Mark said. 'We're just letting you know. Claire needs to take responsibility for her own emotional wellbeing now. She needs to move on.'

His interventions were smugly authoritative; he seemed to have access to some story about their family that Joan didn't have, that wasn't true. What had Claire told him? Joan wanted to shake her, make her admit she'd lied, but she just said, 'Taking responsibility for yourself sounds like a good idea.'

'You should do the same,' Mark said.

Oh, this was too much. This man – who was this man? Why did Claire allow him to speak to her mother like that? Was he an abuser? She started to wonder. Was Claire here under some sort of duress? She wouldn't have assumed that just because of his age, but his behaviour was frightening; it made her frightened for her child.

'Claire,' she said, 'does he talk this way to you?'

'He's sticking up for me. He loves me. This is what it looks like.'

Henry, goaded, said, 'Your Mum's done her best.'

'And what've *you* done?' asked Mark.

Joan quite liked him for that. Joan had always been the baddie where Claire was concerned. Now Henry could get a taste of it, and Joan could rush to his defence more firmly than she'd rush to her own. 'Claire, he's very welcome, but I can't have him speaking to Henry like that.'

Claire gave an ugly laugh that made the two clear cables of snot hanging from her nose lengthen and sway. 'Bully for you,' she said, standing up. 'Come on. It's completely pointless.'

She hobbled out to the car as if she'd just survived a terrible accident, with Mark holding her shoulders. They drove off, and Joan couldn't even see their silhouettes receding, because the back windscreen was entirely blocked by the heap of bags. She and Henry stood there on the gravel for a moment. A blackbird rustled in the hedge. Neither of them spoke. What was there to say? Claire's behaviour, her wild emotion, was so outlandish that once it was over it seemed like a dream.

Turning back to the house, Joan saw movement: the professional couple, standing in the window of room two, staring down as if the private scene had been a form of complimentary entertainment, like the magazines beside their bed.

'Henry,' she said.

He didn't answer. He was standing with his hands on his hips, looking down at the toes of his shoes.

'*Henry.*'

'I just need a minute.'

Joan felt a spot of rain on her cheek. The sky had clouded over; she would have to rescue the sheets from the line. They had a regular due that night, a quiet man, Federico, who stayed every week so he could take his mother to St Margaret's early on Monday morning. Something to do with her lipids. Joan gathered the damp sheets and took them inside and put them in the tumble drier. Then she went upstairs and banged on the door of Room Two. There was a scuffling inside. The girl appeared in a robe, her hair loose.

'Yes?'

'You have to leave.'

The girl's expression was amused, appraising. 'I don't think so. I think we're booked another night.'

'I don't care what you're booked. Get your stuff.'

'Is there a problem?'

'I don't have to explain myself to you,' Joan said. 'This is my house and I don't want either of you in it.'

The girl laughed, a hard, dismayed little laugh, then stopped. 'I'm not paying.'

'Not for tonight, no.'

'Not for last night either. Is this how you run your business? It's pathetic. You wouldn't last a week in a city.'

'You'll pay for the night you stayed. I'll charge your card.'

'Just so you know,' the girl hissed, 'your other daughter's upstairs throwing things. So you're a fabulous mother, too.'

Joan found Tessa's bedclothes ripped off, piles of graphic novels knocked over, broken irreplaceable Victorian tiles on the hearth, but no Tess. The curtains were open. Tessa had a lovely view of the laburnum tree, now bleak and withered like an ancient flay, though in summer its blazing yellow flowers trailed to earth in long chains that shifted in the breeze, revealing vertical slices of the garden, the field where one horse grazed. The childhood Joan had offered them could not have been more idyllic. But what did it matter: what did it matter with girls. Claire had ridden off on the back of her own mood, she'd taken it with her, she'd spread it wherever she went, and Joan would not be permitted to defend herself.

A sharp tap, close by, made her whirl around, absurdly fearing an intruder. But the noise had come from the cupboard. So that was where Tessa had gone. Joan knelt and saw that the door was slightly open, and that the fairy lights, incredibly, were still operational, bathing Tessa in a pale glow as she lay on her back, her feet against the wall, the lights looping and swirling within touching distance above her face, the sloped ceiling receding into the eaves, into darkness.

'Leave me alone,' Tessa said. Her voice was hard, and Joan knew that she must have overheard everything. Tessa had a nasty habit of creeping around the house, listening to conversations that had nothing to do with her.

Joan crawled inside the cupboard; she somehow folded her legs underneath her, twisted around, and pulled the door closed. The sense of pleasure was immediate, primal. A cave. The light from each bulb was sharp, but didn't travel far, and the darkness in the eaves was undisturbed. She could hear her daughter breathing. She wanted to touch her, but knew that Tessa would fight her off. Gently, slowly, she leaned against the door, and felt it click. Felt it hold.

'You didn't shut it properly?' Tessa said, with disbelief.

'What do you mean?'

'Did you close it all the way?'

'Should I not have done that?'

Tessa rolled over and put her hands flat against the door. It didn't move. 'You've locked us in.'

Joan laughed. 'I can't have done.'

'You have. There's no handle inside.'

The door wouldn't give, whatever they tried. Tessa was laughing now, but differently, almost cruelly. She didn't seem to care – she'd brought herself in here, hadn't she? It was where she wanted to be. But Joan had things to do. Federico would be arriving. The lamb needed its rub.

She called for Henry – feebly at first, then louder, though she couldn't bring herself to yell full-throat. It seemed ridiculous. She banged on the door, and the banging drowned her voice out, the tone of it, growing more exasperated now, as if this was all Henry's fault for not listening closely enough. Was he still outside on the gravel? Had he gone to his shed?

'You must have a way to open it,' she said. 'You and Claire, you must have had a way.'

But Tessa lay down and closed her eyes.

Joan heard the dim final sound of a car door slamming – the couple leaving, perhaps. Perhaps it had been stupid to evict them. That girl was the sort who'd write terrible reviews on all the websites she could find. But what was the point of owning your own business, if not to make things personal once in a while? It was not a power Joan had exercised often, but one she'd been glad to possess. A sort of silent compensation.

She tried to remember what she'd learned about the attic when they first moved in. This had been nineteen years ago, when Claire was five or six. She remembered it had needed insulation, a thick layer of fibreglass fluff the contractors laid down, because there were gaps all over the place, spaces for the house's warm air to rise into, then escape between the orange tiles. Hadn't there been some question of obstructing the eaves? The ceiling sloped sharply – the cupboard, the attic, was anvil-shaped – and Joan crawled into the narrowest part of the wedge until she felt cold air on her hands. The inside walls of the cupboard didn't actually meet the external walls of the house. There was space, at the end, to squeeze through, and even to descend, stepping from joist to joist, wriggling down the cavity wall, then – what? Breaking through the plasterboard into the dining room? Making a mess? No, she would not go down. She'd go sideways, towards the other bedroom on the attic floor, which was hers and Henry's.

The end wall scraped her ribs and cheek as she wriggled past; her head bumped a tile, though it didn't fall. There was some kind of space, though it wasn't the other cupboard: it was empty but for yellow insulation and hammocks of spiders' webs and a few spokes of light picking out the disused chimney breast that fed the fireplace in her own room. Nearly there. She crawled across and touched the far wall and found her way to the end.

This time the gap was narrower, and she thought she might not be able to squeeze through at all, and then not be able to squeeze back. She'd be pinned for ever. Tess would never tell; they'd never find her. She'd be like one of those mummified pigeon corpses the man had fished out from behind the electric fire, just a bundle of bones and leathery skin and imperishable jeggings, a cautionary tale for the house's next owner ...

With a last convulsion she was out, though she felt her sleeve tear. She crawled forward. Blocky heaps against the black were the boxes and cases they had piled in there; and strokes of light outlined the cupboard door ahead, which was held with just a catch on the outside, tiny and fragile, she'd break it easily if she pushed, and she did. Daylight burst in, dazzling her. She turned back towards the junk and shouted, 'Tessa, it's all right, I'm through.'

No answer. Little madam. She could wait to be released.

Downstairs there was no sign of Henry. No sign of Richard, either. Joan hoped he hadn't got a puncture. He did that sometimes, got stranded on the moors, and Henry had to drive out and fetch him. Maybe that was where Henry had gone.

She went out on to the driveway, and saw that Henry's car was not there. Neither was the couple's. Neither was Mark's. Claire had gone – she was always going, but she always came back. Joan had once picked her up from the bus stop at the end of the road, to which she had dragged her Winnie-the-Pooh suitcase on its wobbly single wheel. She had collected her from the bus station, too, when the man she'd got obsessed with, a former guest at the B&B, had failed to make good on his promise to spirit her away to France. That had been a long drive home, the hate radiating off her, as if Joan had arranged the betrayal herself, not been scrubbing bathrooms all morning, oblivious to her daughter's absconding from home, from school, until she'd phoned for a lift.

Near the pylon, through the hedge, Joan saw the red flash of a car. Not Henry – his was silver – but Federico, arriving exactly as planned, on a normal Sunday night. Joan went inside to put the kettle on. She always made Federico a cup of tea when he arrived; she would sit with him as he drank it, patiently teasing from him whatever would pass for news, before he went to the carvery up the road. Federico was a nervous speaker, his plumpness rather feminine, his fluttering lashes saving him from meeting anyone's eye, though that didn't stop Joan trying. She thought if she tried, and succeeded, he'd be grateful.

Federico parked carefully, and took his time getting out of the car, retrieving his overnight bag from the back seat, and something else, some sort of soft toy, luridly green. Perhaps his mother was getting senile now, finding comfort in those sorts of things. Or perhaps the toy was his: Joan would not have been surprised to find that Federico slept with something stuffed. Waving through the window, she saw him wave back and head towards the house. She met him at the door.

'Federico, lovely to see you.' She touched her hair: cobwebs and dust. 'We're doing DIY. How are *you*?'

Federico set his bag down on the doorstep and pulled the green toy – an alligator – over his right hand. His fingers entered its snout. They brought it to life. 'Terrible,' he said. The snout moved in time with the syllables; the pink tongue flashed. Federico's voice sounded unusually hoarse, and he was speaking with an accent, presumably Italian – his mother was Italian – that he'd never possessed before. 'I'm sicka this journey. I'm sicka my Mama. How are you?'

'Oh,' Joan said. She was laughing, but she didn't know why. The thing was too odd to strike her as funny. It was too strange that Federico should have brought a puppet along, today, after she'd found that old brochure of Claire's. It was confusing. The feeling the alligator gave her was the same feeling she'd had with Suzanne: that this shouldn't be done in public, that it was silly and puerile, but also somehow danger-ous, somehow kicking at a vital support; and that the kicking was aimed at her, in the end: her inability to get the joke.

'Let me in,' the alligator said.

Joan stirred and stepped back. 'Of course – please, come in.' What else could she say? 'The kettle's on. Henry's nipped out. I don't suppose you saw him when you came up the road?'

Guests were not normally allowed in the kitchen, or the living room, both of which had little signs nailed to the doors that said *Private*, but at some point this had stopped applying to Federico, who was so quiet, so deeply unassuming, that Joan had felt compelled to make an exception for him, to show him that – in this small sense at least – he could be an exceptional man. She poured his tea.

'You not gonna sit down?'

'Oh yes.' Down she sat. Federico held the alligator up on the table. It was watching Joan, who forgot to fetch her own cup, who sat in a daze, not asking questions.

'So you finally decide, don't you,' the alligator said, at last.

'Decide what?'

'Federico. He not worth it.' Joan opened her mouth, but the toy continued. 'It's OK. Most people, they give up quicker than you. You almost make him believing you actually like him!'

'No,' she said, 'that's not— I've had a strange day. And the puppet . . .' It was hard not to look at the alligator, but she made herself look at Federico, his sad, sloping eyes, averted, of course.

'He's giving up on himself, you know. Of course you know. You can sense it. Him and his Mama, for ever. When she's gone there won't be nothing left. It is cruel, though,' the alligator said, 'to change your mind today. You have invite him for dinner – or do you forget?'

She had forgotten.

'No,' she said, 'of course not. I just have to finish making up your room. Would you give me a minute?'

In the utility room, she gathered the warm sheets from the dryer and held them to her chest. Upstairs, she made Federico's bed. Then she went to Tessa's room, to let her out. She was relieved to find the cupboard door still closed. It meant Tessa had not been teasing, had not withheld from her the means of escape. She twisted the handle, and the door released. Tessa was still lying on her back, still gazing up at the wreath of lights, but there was something sitting on her stomach. Joan's heart gave a single massive thump. Tessa turned to look at her. The thing turned too.

'Leave me alone,' it said, in Tessa's deepest voice.

Joan fell backwards away from the cupboard. Somehow she scrambled across the hall towards her own room, shut the door, even locked it – they had a tiny key in the lock they never used, though once upon a time they had turned it if they ever made love – and ran to the far side of the bed, her side, where she sat on the floor, already feeling silly for how she'd reacted. There would be an explanation. Tessa would've found some old toy that Claire had missed. Maybe she'd found Suzanne – though it hadn't been Suzanne. No pink, no white. Joan had seen a dark colour, brownish perhaps, or greenish, like the mould in the bottom of the cups. And a smell. Had there been a smell? Had Tessa been keeping something horrible in there? Why did Joan have to think about this? It was ridiculous, it was unfair, it was nearly Christmas. She ought to be putting the last cards on the mantelpiece and getting the lamb in the oven.

The house had fallen quiet. She would just stay here. Maybe she needed to lie down for a minute. It was not like Joan to lie down in the day, she thought it weak and slovenly, but the circumstances, really, were extraordinary, enough to slip her shoes off and settle on the bed, among the pale decorative cushions that Henry grumbled about having to remove and stack on the love-seat every night.

Muster's Puppets – it was all because she'd found that bloody brochure. She'd got puppets on the brain. They had taken the children on a journey to the moon, but they'd taken the adults, too. She'd sat in the darkness, rolling Richard's pram back and forth, an instinctual rhythm, and watched the puppeteers manoeuvre their spotlit characters into a rocket, then lift them into the air, light as paper, while projected stars wheeled across the back of the stage. Amazing, the capacity to efface themselves, to draw the whole crowd into the story, which was a simple one, of course: of boredom at home, then travel, then adventure that outstripped their appetites for it – the moon puppets looming, their limbs lit blue – and then, at last, the relieved return, and the moon reduced to what it had previously been, just a picture in the sky.

There had been questions, too. One of the puppets, the red one, had asked her friends, the children watching, even and especially the creatures on the moon, what happiness was. The question had obsessed her throughout the show, and the answers changed – of course – depending on who she asked. Her friends said a wonderful book, or a new adventure. The children said it was a tingly feeling, or a sense of being warm. The moon-men responded in a warbling language that she couldn't understand. And when they finally returned, after the moon-men had chased them off, after they had managed to repair their rocket and then to land it again without crashing, they had kissed the ground like demonstrative Americans, and the red puppet had announced that happiness was home.

Joan had not thought of this for years, the papier-mâché moon, and the cheap little tear that had come to her eye, which she'd refused to feel ashamed of, though one of the mothers had smiled at her, slightly condescendingly, when the lights came up. Claire had tried to recreate the red puppet, Joan remembered. That was the point of Suzanne. And something else, too: something Claire had said, that had prompted the confiscation. Joan had marched Claire out of the breakfast room, where she was, it was true, bothering the guests at breakfast, asking silly questions in Suzanne's silly voice – asking them, maybe, what *they* thought happiness was – and she'd told Claire that if she didn't stop it there was going to be trouble. But Claire hadn't yielded. She'd looked at Suzanne, and Suzanne had looked at Joan, its eyes goggling, and said, 'You don't have any happiness. It doesn't want to live with you.'

Funny, in a way, in retrospect. Little girls don't know what they're saying. They misbehave, they're punished, they let fly with some new language to express their rage, and it's all forgotten in the space of an hour. Joan didn't respond, except to put Suzanne in the cupboard; but she didn't forget, or not completely. Wasn't she remembering now?

Joan heard a footstep – someone outside. The door rattled. A pause; another attempt; then: 'Joan? Have you locked the door?'

It was Henry – his normal voice. 'Henry? Is that you?'

'It's me,' he said. 'Let me in.'

She ran and touched the little key, and was almost impressed with herself, with her body, to see her hand shaking. The chemicals, adrenaline – they worked. It was all so ridiculous, but when it was happening, how were you to know? Better to have the reaction and feel like an idiot later than stand paralysed and disbelieving while something went wrong.

'I fetched Richard,' Henry said. 'We brought a takeaway.'

So much for the lamb. But that didn't matter. He'd brought dinner, he was here, he was sorting it out. Kind, dependable Henry. He would forgive her – he always did. The key turned, and the door came open. There he was, in his waterproof jacket, with a puppet on his hand: some sort of shaggy doggy beast the same silver as his hair.

'What on earth have you been doing?' asked the beast, but it was Henry, it was Henry's own voice. Inside its mouth was a circle of pink felt.

'You're all having fun with me, aren't you?' Joan cried. 'You're all in on it together. Is it meant to be a joke? Was it Claire's idea?'

'What's going on?'

'Stop waving that thing around, Henry, or God help me, I will rip it off your hand.'

'Federico said you were acting strangely. He said you'd lost your voice.'

Hearing this, Joan thought quite calmly that she might have gone mad. Wasn't that what madness was – believing in a version of events that didn't tally with the versions of others? Seeing the innards of your head in the world outside?

'Where've you put it?' the Henry-beast asked.

'Where've I put *what*?' Joan asked angrily, but she thought she knew what he meant. He meant Suzanne. Fine. If that was what they all wanted, Joan would find it. She ducked inside the cupboard and put the light on. The stacks of boxes, untouched for nearly twenty years, the cracked old suitcases and soft bags stuffed in between them, materialised. There were plenty of black bin bags, too, but when Joan started opening them they only held ancient yellowed duvets or underwhelming Halloween costumes, like the acre of torn-up sheets she'd once wound with a patience now unimaginable around Richard's pyjama'd limbs. Maybe she should stay in the cupboard, with the things she remembered ranged solidly around her, until whatever was happening came to an end.

'The food's getting cold,' Henry called.

Suzanne was not in any of the bags. Despairing, she opened a box, and saw her mother's cutlery. She opened another and it was full of crumpled yellow newspaper with nestled inside it three of the Toby jugs. Their faces stared up at her, rigid and rosy with gin. The central jug was the one she reached for. This, unusually, was a woman: a stout, matronly figure with bloated cheeks and a dark blue tricorne hat, out of which – had you used the jug as a jug, which Joan's mother never did – the liquid would have poured. There had only been two women in her mother's collection. The rest of them, twenty-five or so, had been middle-aged men, some drinking, some with pipes or snuff, all squatting in the glass-fronted cabinet that dominated the dining room, their bulbous glazed chins and bellies shining. The blue woman had been the only jug that had ever appealed to Joan, though she couldn't say she'd liked her. It was more of a fascinated fear.

She picked her up and marched her back to Henry. 'There. Is this what you want?'

Henry smiled – he almost looked relieved. 'All right. Let's go.'

The sweetish smell of Chinese food struck her as she passed through the door. There they all were, arranged around the kitchen table like a family photograph just waiting to be taken: Federico with his alligator, Richard with a carved wooden knickerbockered boy, Tessa with her rotten animate compost heap shedding dark filaments on to the floor, Neal – since when had Neal arrived? – with a faceless lump like a cricket sock packed with dough, and Claire, terrible Claire, her face inside the raised hood of the black cagoule still swollen from crying, holding up the buoyant dome of Suzanne's head, its rice-cake-rubbled surface. One of the goggly eyes had fallen off, but the other adhered and swivelled, looking at Joan with old dislike.

Henry joined them, turning the Henry-beast to face his wife. They were all expectant: they wanted her to speak. Presumably she was meant to use the Toby jug. She lifted it, the pottery cool in her hands, rough at the lip where the glaziery stopped. The Toby-woman's mouth could not be manipulated, but Joan could bob the jug up and down as she talked.

'Well,' she began, then stopped. Her voice was meant to change, wasn't it? Only Henry's had stayed the same. Poor transparent Henry. He didn't get the joke. She was only just beginning to get it herself.

She pushed her tongue down and narrowed her throat and aspirated hard to get a wheezy sort of sound, like her mother in the later stages of emphysema – a sound she'd never forgotten, but never attempted to reproduce. What she wanted to say was how *glad* she was to have them all home for Christmas, and that although a Chinese takeaway wasn't exactly what she'd had in mind – it was meant to be lamb, she'd got a very good lamb shank from the butcher's – that really didn't matter, because they were all together, and that's what counts. But what issued from her mouth were wheezing vowels, long and painful, with no stops, no consonants, in between. The family was still watching, but they looked dismayed.

'What's wrong with her?' the Tessa-monster asked.

'She's lost her voice,' said the Neal-sock.

'I haven't,' Joan insisted, 'I'm talking,' but the words came out as more wheezing, which they all ignored.

'What should we do?'

'Where could it be?'

'Has she *swallowed* it?'

'Yes, yes!' It was Suzanne, on Claire's arm, who rose from the table. 'She must have swallowed her voice. We'll have to look for it.'

Taking up one of the table knives, Claire advanced.

A SOURCE

The next editor of the university newspaper was chosen each year by a panel made up of the current editor, deputy editor, managing editor, news editor and cultural editor of the paper, the current president of the Students' Union and his or her press officer, the current president of the Journalism Society, plus any number of undeclared presences. No formal applications were invited. The criteria, if they existed, were undisclosed. Nominations would be made at the start of Trinity term, and by the end of it someone would be anointed. There was a rumour that the favourite would be whoever delivered the best story in that narrow window, and looking back through the archive it was possible to see that the appointment was more often than not preceded by a scoop.

Claire thought a lot about this. It was silly, obviously. It was just a student newspaper. She knew that. At the same time, they were encouraged to take things seriously here. And Claire was good; she'd be a good editor. She believed totally in the paper's ethos, which was a kind of piratical liberalism – anti-capital, anti-Israel, pro-legalisation, pro-choice – though conservative tastes were tolerated on the arts pages. There had never been a female editor before.

'One guy,' she told her mother on the phone, 'one guy wrote this story about how two of the colleges employed a contractor who donates to the BNP to build their new halls. The colleges tried to pretend they hadn't known about it, but this guy showed that they *must* have known. He's on staff at the *Independent* now.'

'Oh, the *Independent*,' said her mother. 'They'd like that kind of thing.'

The nominations were announced with Canada goose feathers: Claire found one stapled to her name on the newsroom wall after Easter. She took the feather down as if it were an eagle's pinion, not something dropped from the dirty backside of one of the geese now so populous on the riverside that they were not in any sense exotic, as they must have been when the tradition began. Ben, the editor, put his hands on her shoulders and shook her very firmly. Others clapped who had hoped to be tipped themselves. Duncan was one.

'Sorry,' she said, in the Queen's Head afterwards.

'Why're *you* sorry?' he said. 'They're the ones who should be sorry. Stuck-up bastard cunts. I think I might finally've had enough of this place.'

Duncan was from Stoke-on-Trent, and Claire loved him a little bit, although she couldn't tell whether this was because of who he was, intrinsically, or because they had spent so much time together, working on proofs or essays until 2am in Duncan's room, him at the desk and Claire curled on his single bed, eventually falling asleep there rather than set out on the long walk back to the centre.

Duncan was reading History. Claire was reading English. Neither was happy to say they were 'reading' any subject at all, but while Claire gritted her teeth and saw it through, Duncan's bitter discomfort made him generate countless alternatives, all equally absurd.

'*I'm* knowing History,' he'd say, in his cattiest voice. 'What are *you* knowing?'

Claire, catching on, would say, '*I'm* knowing English.'

'Oh, how *marvellous*,' he would reply.

They had met at the freshers' fair, signing up for the paper. Duncan wore black skinny jeans that made his legs look like liquorice sticks, and a navy wool duffel coat with huge pockets. His skin was bad, his hair unwashed; he looked dirty and sullen and proud, as if he had just survived six months at sea. When she'd said this to him later, in a moment of drunken exuberant disburdening, he'd said, 'No, you're thinking of a reefer jacket.'

Claire had borrowed that coat innumerable times, and even fallen asleep on it. It was scratchy, and it smelled of damp tobacco. The pockets had holes in the corners that coins dropped through – you could feel them around the hem, like tiny weights.

She set about trying to find a story, the right story, but her only idea was college catering: kitchen wastage; unfairly tendered contracts with suppliers; the astonishing predominance of processed carbohydrates in students' meals. Sub-par nourishment for over-par brains! It was ridiculous. She complained one morning to June, the scout for the building, when June came to clean Claire's room and found her listless and afraid.

'Oh, I could tell you some things about this place,' June said breezily. She had violet-coloured pouches beneath her eyes, and hair that did not seem to be subject to gravity at all, that floated around her face like a puff of seed.

'Like what?' Claire asked. Other girls in the building didn't talk to June much, but Claire found it easy. June was like her aunties; she was like the women who'd worked in the offices at her school, where half the buildings were prefabricated, like builders' huts. There was a kind of ease between them that Claire felt proud of being able to create.

'Like you wouldn't believe,' June said. 'Bursars stealing then buggering off. Shahs getting their kids in without the proper qualifications, just talking to the principal and making a big donation the same year. The roof on this building came from a shah!'

'How d'you know?'

'His daughter told me. She had the room down the hall. Never picked up her clothes neither, never did a damn thing, and then she used to lie there while I was hoovering and watch. Lovely eyes. She used all that eyeliner, like they do.'

'That's amazing,' Claire said. Imagine! She would have to go digging into the donors' list, and then she'd have to cross-reference it with the alumni roll, and even then it might not be clear.

'Once there was this amateur cricket club over from – I don't know where, Malaysia or something …'

Might there be something about the new roof in the college newsletter? It was exactly the kind of thing they'd want to boast about.

'… then it was later that day, I was in cleaning the loos upstairs, and he just appeared in the doorway.'

'Who did?'

'This chap I'd turned down. He'd got his cricket whites on, and there were these big green grass stains all down his front, right down to his knees. He was just standing there, watching me clean.'

Claire felt a prickling along her arms.

'I didn't know what he wanted at first, but I knew it wasn't right, something wasn't right. He was blocking the doorway. So I just said, oh, hello, how are you, then I tried to go past him, but maybe that was what he wanted. He got me up against the wall, you know, by the throat.'

'What did you do?'

'Well, I just thought, that's it, I'm going to be strangled by a Malaysian chap in the loos! Then he – you know, he did what he wanted to do, I suppose. Then somebody came past at one point, and he let go a bit, and I got away from him and ran downstairs and went straight over to the lodge, looking for my manager, you know. He was sitting in there eating this big plate of chips from the canteen. I told him what had happened and he said, That's terrible, June, but you do know the cricketers are going home tomorrow, don't you? So you won't have to see him again.'

She laughed in a bewildered sort of way, and started emptying Claire's bin.

'But June,' Claire said. 'That's horrendous.'

'Oh, I know it is, I know, but what can you do?'

'I don't know, but there has to be *something*. Nothing was done? Really nothing at all?'

Oh no, June said, nothing ever got done. It was just the job, wasn't it? And other things happened to other scouts in other colleges. Abuse from the students: things thrown at them, or horrible things left in the rooms for them to find. Assaults by the students, too. Sexual assaults. Exposing themselves. But that all got hushed up.

'I don't know,' she said. 'Maybe that's just how it has to be. They're just young lads, after all, aren't they? They don't really know what they're doing.'

Claire felt dizzy, dazzled with unfairness. June carried on talking for the both of them. Anyway, she was saying, most of them weren't like that, most of them were good as gold. Chocolates at the end of the term, sometimes, and a thank-you card. Once in a while, some of them even came back for a visit. She'd had one lad who'd called her Second Mum. That was before she moved to the women's college, of course. Girls didn't tend to do that sort of thing. They were much more reserved. She missed the lads sometimes. You couldn't really wish a criminal record on them, could you? Not at that age.

When June busied off down the corridor, Claire typed up everything she could remember of the conversation, of June's form of words. She didn't put June's name on it. She didn't know if June would want to be named. She'd have to find that out. Her mind was swarming. Imagine breaking this! Oh, and she was angry, she was angry too, on June's behalf and all the other scouts' behalves – but she had to focus.

She opened a new document and began to draft the story. Should it be about the incident itself and the college's failure to investigate? Or should it be bigger, wider – endemic sexual assault, fear of constructive dismissal? Excitement carried her a long way, through the next hour or two. It would go national, surely. There was an insatiable appetite for stories about the university in the national press, especially with sexual assault in the mix. And what happened to June had been serious. It had maybe been – probably – rape. But lack of attribution or corroboration: that could be a problem.

She phoned Duncan. 'How well do you get on with your scout?' There was a rustling sound, a groan. 'You're still in bed, aren't you?'

'I am resting,' Duncan said. His voice was muffled. 'I fucking hate that word.' He meant *scout*. Claire hated it too, if she thought about it. As if the cleaners weren't employed, were just gleeful volunteers, overgrown children, who cleaned toilets for nothing more than the privilege of attaining little coloured badges of experience to sew on to their overalls. And yet there was something appealing about it, too. The term *scout* was itself a little badge, one that Claire had been proud to collect.

'I know,' she said, 'I know, but can I talk to her?'

'Is this for your article? You've gone off catering and now you're on cleaning?'

'Something like that,' she said, cagily. Duncan's scout was Duncan's, after all.

Irina was a morose Polish girl with no shoulders and a tiny gold cross in her clavicle notch.

'I don't know nothing about that,' she said, emptying Duncan's bin of chocolate wrappers and tinfoil from the kebab van, the orange grease clinging to it. She tutted. 'Rubbish you eat!'

'Claire was gonna write something about that, weren't you?' Duncan said. 'About all the rubbish we eat round here.'

'Yes! These students don't eat no vegetables, they don't drink no water, it's all kebabs and chocolate and beer, all the time. It's crazy. Why do you want to come here to work so hard and feed your brains with all that rubbish? This is what you should write.'

'But Irina, these other stories, you haven't heard anything like that?'

Irina snorted. 'Of course. If it's men, if it's women' – she made a strange gesture with her left hand – 'that's what happens.'

'Has it happened to you?'

'They tried, but I'm not having none of that.'

'Who tried?'

'Why'm I gonna tell you that? I'm not gonna tell you that. This is my job. You think they go after the students who pays them nine thousand pound a year? No, they go after me, they get rid of me. And there's nobody else gonna talk to you about this, either.'

'Actually, someone has.'

She felt Duncan look sharply at her, and ignored him.

Irina's small mouth twisted and released a contemptuous laugh. 'What idiot's gonna talk to you about that?' She turned to Duncan. 'You got any more rubbish in here?' And when he said no, she left, abruptly, with the transparent sac spinning by one stretched handle from her thumb.

Duncan was still looking at Claire. 'She hasn't given you permission, has she? Whoever she is.'

Claire approached other scouts at her college the next day, but found them unwilling even to chat about ordinary things. The story sat open on her laptop, unattributed, glowing with power. It distracted her from *Measure for Measure* so much that she had to write her essay before she'd finished reading the text. She expected the tutor to humiliate her for this, but he seemed half-asleep, and in fact only corrected her very mildly on a few points, as if he'd never anticipated anything better from her. She trudged back to her building, past the girls lying out on the lawns. The pages of their magazines glistened in the grass; their hair fell forward around their faces, and she could almost smell their shampoo: coconut and synthetic apples.

She got herself a Diet Coke, and as it clunked out of the vending machine she saw June pass by with her cleaning kit, humming to herself. She followed her upstairs to the communal kitchen, and found her cleaning the hobs.

'I still can't believe it,' Claire said, watching June closely. 'What happened to you.'

'Oh, don't be silly,' June replied. She had reached a tough bit of something unidentifiable, once onion, perhaps, now blackened, oily and welded to the burner, and she was having to press down on her knot of steel wool with both hands to try and dislodge it. The effort seemed immense. Claire started forward, as if to help, just as the clot gave way.

'Look at that.' June pinched it between her yellow-gloved fingertips and held it up as if it was a dead spider. 'That's been cooked about six times, that has. It's their noodles. Honestly, they wouldn't ever think to clean up.'

By 'they', she meant the Chinese students, who always fed themselves in teams of four or six, filling the whole kitchen with steaming pans. Anything that looked like a noodle June attributed to them, though Claire had never once seen them cook noodles: they seemed to favour packets of readymade tortellini and ravioli, which they boiled up and covered in butter and parmesan and ate with forks at the communal table. June's casual racism had not bothered Claire the other day, when June mentioned the shah's daughter. It had seemed like something speaking through her, not something she had chosen for herself. But first the shah, then the Malaysian chap, now this: June was othering them – and openly, too. Did she imagine that she and Claire had this in common?

'The rest of the girls were just like you,' June said, talking on regardless. 'All cross and saying I ought to do something. But you think that when it's someone else, don't you? You think it was probably worse than it was.'

'What if they come back? What if he does it to someone else?'

'Oh, they haven't been back for years. They won't be back now, I don't think.'

She had started cleaning the sink. The hot water ran hard against the stainless steel.

'I think that's a bit irresponsible, actually,' Claire cried, above the tropical noise. 'Have you seen the college articles? They're very clear about sexual misconduct.'

June pressed her hand against her side, as if she were climbing a hill and had got a stitch. She turned off the tap. 'This plughole's blocked. I'd better get the thingamajig.'

Claire waited, inspecting the sink, which didn't seem blocked at all. The water drained; she saw her face in the bottom, a pink smear. Arguments came to her: that women have a responsibility to each other to speak up when it counts; that June's coming forward, in whatever form, might be exactly what someone else needed to hear. But all she could see was June's puffball hair blowing this way and that, never settling, never touching down, catching the breeze and tumbling June sideways out of the room.

Really, it was more than racism speaking through her. It was sexism too, it was all kinds of ingrained obliviousnesses, ones Claire didn't have time to correct. The story would wriggle away from her. It would jump, like an unhooked fish, and nobody, nobody, was ever going to catch it again, because June – she could tell – had scared herself, or Claire had scared June with how seriously she had taken her allegations.

Then why did she tell me? she thought, angrily. Why did she tell me at all? And it occurred to her that maybe, as far as June was concerned, she'd done her part. Who was to say she'd not already given her permission as she understood it? Maybe she thought Claire was pestering her to append her name to the piece, or to identify the man. Maybe she wanted Claire to go and write the damn thing regardless, with minimal contact, so that June could later deny responsibility for it, like a real confidential informant. She had told Claire, after all. She must have known what Claire was doing.

For a moment it seemed to Claire that she, herself, might even be part of the problem. It was a thought she did not enjoy: it seemed almost to encroach upon her space, like someone unwanted, a drunk, sitting beside you on a train. She left the Coke on the counter and went back to her room. The only way out was to jump, the way June had jumped in telling Claire the truth. Then they would be standing on the other side of the decision, and things would look different there. She just had to send the email – so she did.

She had a long shower that stayed hot all the way through, that beat her skin till it pinked and glowed. Journalists shouldn't expect to be liked. Duncan had told her that. Back in her room, she texted him: *Drink?* The building was terribly quiet, and she dived on her phone when it rang.

'Claire, it's Ben! Is this real?' He was shouting against a hundred voices that seemed to be ramming themselves down the phone. He was where life was. That was the sound of life. 'It's fucking amazing. Are you around? We're at the Union. Can you come down?'

Yes, she said, she'd go, she'd be there soon. Still no word from Duncan. She texted him again: *Going to the Union. C u there?* He wouldn't come. He didn't like the Union. Too many sherry-sippers. Too much black tie and coke in the toilets and chalets in Megève. It bothered him, he said, it being called the *Union* when it was the total exact fucking opposite of what that word meant, and for a long time she'd avoided it, wanting Duncan's approval. Now she wanted Ben to greet her approvingly, too, like a prospect; like an equal. She wanted him to say her story was fucking amazing to her face. And even once it came out, once Duncan stopped talking to her altogether, once June stopped coming to work and another scout took over, and Claire returned from a tutorial one day to find her bed full of rubbish, actual rubbish, wet and stinking orange peel and yoghurt pots and clumped spaghetti in tomato sauce and the chewed end of a kebab, and she had to bundle it all up inside the sheet and carry it to the kitchen, a disgusting baby – even then, she knew that she wanted these things.

PLIGHT

For a long time, Claire maintained that if you got to know someone – anyone – very well, then you would come to love them, in a sense. Love was a factor of familiarity. It didn't much matter what you were becoming familiar *with*. There needn't be things in common.

The figure she used to illustrate this, at university and beyond, was her elder brother, Callum. She and Callum, by anyone's reckoning, were not alike. Claire was reading Art History as a pretext for drinking too much and, when she could afford it, taking cocaine. Her friends in halls knew her as a sleepless lock-in attender, a last-minute essay basher-out, and when she invited them, in the Union bar, to imagine what this elder brother was like, they pictured someone equally reckless. But Callum worked for the genetics service on Ward 10 of Chapel Allerton Hospital, karyotyping patients' chromosomes in order to reveal the trisomies that were caus-ing recurrent miscarriage. He wore Levi 550s in medium stonewash that he bought once a year from the outlet at McArthurGlen. He wasn't autistic, he just hated shopping. If he had been born in 1400, he might have become an itinerant preacher, crying *Vanity of vanities, all is vanity!* in the streets.

She wanted to theorise her bond with her family as an accident of exposure: the same brick semi-detached, barbecue and swingball set. Mum and Dad and Callum and her and Dean.

Dean was the youngest. Claire was in the middle. Callum, the crown prince, had lived four years before his sister came along, with their mother all to himself. He was not spoilt in any obvious way. His demands were infrequent and modest: that he could be allowed to stay up to watch *The Crystal Maze*; that he not have to play sports any more. Their father thought there was something maladapted about him. Look at those shoulders: he was born for rugby. He'd got a strategic mind. Why on earth did he want to hide in his bedroom painting figurines?

Claire assumed the intermediary position on this. She spent Saturdays at her friends' houses, trying on their clothes, envying and fancying their sportive brothers, and even, sometimes, their dads. But on Sunday afternoons she stayed at home and sprawled on her stomach on the tough grey carpet of Callum's room, playing with the figures he had sanded, primed and painted so elaborately, with such steady-handed care, then placed among the armies that covered his flocked polystyrene hills. Each figure stood upon a plastic base the size of a 1p coin, and Callum had glued a circle of felt to every one.

Claire had written her final dissertation on the subject of felt. The choice had been a panicked one, made on the morning of the title deadline; but later it had come to seem preternaturally wise, allowing her to dwell on the remembered pleasures of those fuzzy-felt bases clinging to the scabrous landscape, and the stuffed decoy birds of prey wired to her parents' damson trees, which had seemed so much more covetable for being out of reach.

After university she found bar work and hunted for graduate jobs in the day, application after application, none of which got her anywhere, until a girl she knew hooked her up with a small gallery in need of an intern. It sold, predominantly, textiles: silk wall hangings, feathered dreamcatchery assemblages that wafted in the draft when you opened the door. A little bell rang; the owner came forth, a stout, bouffant-haired woman named Andrea, who wore the collars of her shirts popped up, and permitted Claire to sleep on a roll-away bed in the storage room until she could find a real place to live. It was meant to be her start in curation, but she soon discovered that she was there primarily to dust and pour wine, both things she could already do. Andrea's bourgeois friends, who formed the gallery's only customer base, wanted their art to match their curtains. Sometimes, if she could not sleep, she would come down into the exhibition space, pour herself a glass, and pull loose threads from the works' raw edges, half-hoping to get caught.

One night she boarded the last TransPennine to Leeds and went to see Callum. It was after midnight when she got to his

FRANCES LEVISTON

house. The journey had sobered her up, she thought, except that she was ringing the bell before she realised he might be out. Didn't he have more of a life these days? But the light came on. He was home; he was up.

'Claire?' he said, almost suspiciously, as if she was in disguise. 'Haven't you got work tomorrow?'

'I think I'm going to quit.'

It occurred to her that he could refuse entry. She hadn't seen him for several months. He might have changed – become stronger, less compliant. That would have been worth travelling for. She was thinking this even as he ushered her into the kitchen and put the kettle on. As it bubbled and shook, she realised she knew the rhythm of it, when it would shut itself off.

'Is that the one from home?'

He shrugged. Of course it was. He would take anything their parents offered. All the large furniture in his house was brand new, but what filled the shelves and windowsills were objects he had grown up gazing at. She wondered what was left at her parents' house, whether it would be less haunting to visit them. Behind his glasses, his eyes were red and piggy. He wouldn't sit down, but neither would he say that he wanted to go to bed. It annoyed her so much that she said, 'Shall we watch a film or something?'

They dug out *Fargo* and settled themselves in his front room, where a large framed *Lord of the Rings* poster hung above the couch. That was what growing up meant to Callum. You didn't put away your childish things – you just paid to get them framed. He fell asleep in his chair when Frances

178

McDormand was analysing the footprints in the snow. Claire kept watching as far as the wood-chipper. Then she switched it off, which woke him up.

There was a spare room she could stay in, and a scratchy old pink and yellow beach towel for her, which had been to Tenerife with them, and Devon, and everywhere else. The PC on the corner desk was humming; its mouse mat was branded with a logo of whirling blue blobs in solar system formation.

'God,' she said, 'you're still doing that?'

She nudged the mouse. The interface was different, but she recognised the field of multicoloured radio waves, and the language – things like curve-fitting and doppler drift – from long ago.

'It's been years,' she said. 'Hasn't it been like fifteen years?'

He said, 'That's not a reason to stop.'

Callum had done the SETI thing right from the start, running downloaded data packets through the software he installed on his desktop PC. They wanted at least two hours a week from their volunteers, but Callum was committed: he did way more than that. The world was still on dial-up then, and the shriek of the modem became, in Claire's mind, the unimaginable blurt of an alien vocalisation.

'What are the chances?' she'd ask, excited. Usually he scowled, but once he said, 'You don't know about the Drake equation? The smallest possible number of communicating technological civilisations in the galaxy, the smallest *possible* number, is two.'

Electrified, she watched the screen for what seemed like hours, until the scrolling numbers, the unpleasing monochromatic display, drained the thrill out of her again.

'I'm bored,' she complained, putting her head on the desk. 'There's nothing to do. It just runs by itself. There isn't even anything to see.'

'Go away, then,' Callum replied.

He did not mind boredom; he did not mind relegation to an observer's, a donor's, role. There was something noble in the ingloriousness of unrewarded, anonymous service. The achievements of the individual could not equal those of the masses, and mass achievements demanded this kind of sacrifice. He was scathing of any desire for distinction: he despised genius theory, notions of self-actualisation, or anything else that might delude a person into thinking they were special. He liked to shock her with this perspective. Their parents too. He liked to say things like, When you look at worms, do the worms have different faces? He ate whole apples, pips and all. Sometimes he even ate orange peel, the bitter pith a peculiar satisfaction.

These were harmless shocks; others were more obviously self-destructive. When Callum had been lurking at the top of his pay grade at the hospital for two years, he was offered a promotion – manager of his team – and turned it down. Her father told her that, his neck flaming with irritation. He said, 'What the hell was he thinking?'

Her mother pretended to be shocked as well. She patted Callum on the arm, chastising him indulgently, saying things like, 'Isn't he *stubborn*?'

Claire's mother considered the children her main employment, but she had also worked as a palliative care nurse for fifteen years at Leeds General, and later, once Dean had gone to school, she'd worked at the hospice up the road, where she washed and fed and drugged the cancer-wasted, the cancer-betrothed, easing their passage into whatever it was that came next, the nature of which she considered it unprofessional to speculate upon. It was also unprofessional to discuss her work: even after retirement, she kept an impenetrable vault of secrets. If asked about it, she would purse her lips, seeming not to think Claire was fit to hear it, not a reliable keeper of the flame; or as if she suspected some form of prurience. Claire began to suspect prurience in herself. She stopped asking. After that, she was thrown a few scraps, a few tantalising comments, almost as if her mother missed the chance to perform her discretion. Once she had said that sometimes people were in too much pain to die.

Felt is not made in an orderly fashion. It comes into being violently, haphazardly, under duress, with only basic elements – fibres, and soap, and water. You can even forget the soap. Felt is unclean. It's the snarls in dogs' coats that the vet shaves off. It's the mats that form in the back of your hair where it rubs against the pillow when you're fucking.

Once Claire dreamed that she and Callum were lovers. In the gloom of the bedroom at the back of their parents' house, they held one another. She had looked at his face so long as a child, she could see it as a lover might, magnified and flushed. The heavy goose-down duvet smothering them was soaked with the anxiety sweat of furtive sex. His eyes, without glasses, were obscene.

She had woken up shaken and defiled. It wasn't just that her brain had concocted such a scenario, in such oppressive detail. It was that the scenario had, in a sense, happened. She felt as if it had. She possessed a memory of it. And hadn't the psychic materials that went into making it up been harvested from something real?

Also in the dream: her mother's footsteps on the landing outside the door, prowling somehow, leaning in, weighing up whether to intrude ... The prospect of her discovering them had been the worst element of all. Claire could take her own shame, but not her mother's.

In the morning, Callum looked exactly the same, drained and bleary, as if he hadn't slept at all. He started fumbling with the toaster and putting pots of jam on the table.

'You don't need to do that,' Claire said, annoyed at the formality. 'I can stand at the counter like anyone else.' He didn't stop. The butter came out, the French press for a pot of real coffee. His hatred of ceremony could sometimes manifest itself in a rigid adherence to domestic ritual. Claire, knowing exactly where he'd keep his open bag of coffee, went to the freezer and fished it out.

'Do you think you'd better ring the gallery?' he asked.

That too: the insistence on ordinary courtesy, even for those who didn't deserve it. Perhaps especially for them.

'They're not paying me properly, you know.'

'But you did agree—'

'They're not paying me properly, so they're exploiting me. And it's boring. What? You think I ought to apologise to them or something? They ought to apologise to *me*.'

A gurn of disapproval crossed the deliberate blandness of his face. She'd wanted that. Let him see her ego, her imperiousness; how much freer she was than him.

Once upon a time, her plan had been to be the big sibling he had never been for her: the one who breaks the pattern; who shows the way. But coming home from university that first summer, she'd found that Callum's conversation had become so aggressively banal that she could hardly stand to talk to him. It was like he'd sworn off saying anything remotely interesting ever again – as if he wanted to present only the smoothest, sheerest, most purchaseless front. She wished she could say that she had chipped away at this, but she hadn't. She'd felt mulish about it. Fucked if she was going to be interesting for *him*.

When they were kids, everything Callum said had been amusing. One Easter they had stayed at a purpose-built holiday village in the Yorkshire Dales, with log cabins, tennis courts, 'entertainments', a simmering green swimming pool that stank of disinfectant, and perimeter fencing, 'for the safety of our guests', that ran between what looked like wooden watchtowers in the trees.

'Look,' Callum had said, pointing out the towers on the first afternoon. 'If ve do not participate, ve vill be shot!'

All of them had laughed at this: Claire for real, Dean in imitation, her parents with anxious bonhomie. Callum had been off school for two weeks – not suspended, not poorly, just *off* – and there was a force field of nervous tension surrounding him, demanding gentle treatment. Nobody told Claire why. Perhaps other sisters would have pressed to know more, but she was content with the facts she was given, like a cat with its ounce of dry food. She had also been content to collaborate in the story that the force field had vanished once Callum returned to school, even as they all continued to live beneath its shining dome.

One of the myths concerned Noah, who herded all the animals into his ark, and these animals – sheep and goats and horses and rabbits and camels and llamas and dogs – all shed their coats and fleeces on the floor, and pissed and shat and trampled on them, so that when the ark finally reached land again and Noah herded the animals off, he discovered that the decks were carpeted in a homogenous mongrel felt.

Alone with Callum in his bright raw box of a house, she wondered if this would be the day when she finally raised with him the subject of his pain. It seemed to her that Callum *was* in pain: chronic, not acute; diffuse, not defined; a deep, unshakeable discomfort with himself, from which he had sought relief only in pitiful, disabling ways.

Exactly how much pain she could not determine. Whatever it was kept him low, but arrogant; it gave him a powerful sense of self that was composed almost entirely of absences and negations; and it both invited her attention and made him impossible to approach, like rolls of glittering concertina wire on top of a wall.

Had she suggested to Callum that he might be depressed, even suicidal, he would have looked at her with pity and contempt, as if she had tried to tell him that his head was on the wrong way around, or had been replaced by something outlandish: a pineapple, or an octopus. This was not necessarily a reason to duck the conversation. She might find it reassuring – his scorn was very firm, after all. But she never tried. She never said it.

Sometimes she sat there, facing him, like this, over a meal, thinking, 'I really ought to ask him about it. What if I don't, and something happens?' But there was a counterbalancing fear in her that saying it would *make* it happen. Maybe what he remained unconscious of could do him no real harm. Or maybe there was nothing to be conscious *of*. Maybe he was just a melancholy, ironic person, but not dangerously so. Maybe his closeness to his mother was natural; Claire's distance the unnatural thing.

Or maybe, she thought, maybe it was simply that she did not love him after all. You could get to know someone very well and still not love them. Familiarity bred – not contempt, but involvement. Implication. Love was something else: a free radical, a roaming grace that could not be predicted or deliberately produced.

Another myth: that Saint Clement and Saint Christopher, banished from Rome to the Chersonesus, tucked scraps of breakwool they found caught on thorns along the way into the soles of their sandals and under the straps to stop the pressure blistering their skin.

If he was going to do it, he would do it as cleanly and unobtrusively as possible. He would not risk harming anyone in the process. Jumping was out. Hanging was too distressing for whoever discovered the body. Certain pills would have launched him gently downstream without catastrophic organ failure and all its attendant emissions, but he could not obtain them without getting the hospital pharmacist into trouble. Claire thought that he would probably go for the car in the garage. He would know how to tape the length of hose tightly into the exhaust, how to stuff the open window with wet towels. He would put on a CD that he liked – *Automatic for the People*, perhaps – and wait for the nausea to pass. The timing of this absention would be very important. It would be done at night, when nobody was likely to interrupt; and that night would be in spring, when there were no birthdays on the horizon. All these provisions would be made with a pathological altruism that bore no meaningful relationship to kindness.

Claire could imagine it fully, even and including how she might respond herself. Regret would feature largely, not least because of the anticipatory nature of her imaginings. She would have endless corridors of that to walk down; endless recursive self-accusations. How could she be here, projecting all this, and not even try to stop it? It wasn't just an unwillingness to credit her own assessment. There was something else – a deeper sort of helplessness; a code of powerless witnessing that she had been given to absorb, whereby the family had all of them silently pledged not to interfere in one another's pain.

Callum was looking at her now, and Claire thought for a moment, idiotically, that he was going to raise the subject himself; but instead he asked, with an illegible twitch of his mouth, 'Have you spoken to Dean?'

Dean, the youngest, had refused even to consider university. He said he wanted to be out in 'the real world', which turned out to consist of ripped films and nightclubs and MDMA and bright white trainers with the laces tucked in, each foreign element an effort to appear less middle class than he was. On Fridays and Saturdays he stayed out all night; he crashed on friends' floors in privately rented ex-council houses on the other side of the city, which his parents knew only because he would phone on Sunday lunchtime and ask to be collected. Claire, when present, had dreaded these calls: the strangled fury they induced in her father, who would wrench the Mondeo out of the drive and zoom off down the road, while her mother wrung her hands and moaned, 'I hope they don't fight . . .'

Retrieved, deposited, sullen and reeking, Dean would make himself sandwiches with a whole packet of premium bacon, then retire to his bedroom, which was, by some historical and unremedied accident of allocation, the biggest in the house. That was the problem, Claire thought. They had given him too much room: even after they bought him a pool table to fill some floor space, he continued to bounce around the walls. Rebellious, they said. Rebelling against his Dad. But that was still acceptable, could still be understood, because his rebellion had been mounted from within the allegedly rejected sphere.

The baize on that pool table had haunted Claire's dissertation: grass-green worsted glued to planes of wood composite, turning what would have been the sharp sound of the heavy hurtling balls into a muted rumble that ran down the table's legs and vanished into the floor. The hours they spent leaning on their cues, intent upon, obsessed with, the game. The utter infuriation of never being able to strike a ball directly; having always to strike the cue ball first, its ivory colour creating what Claire had taken for an optical illusion that it was larger than the rest . . .

Though Dean still technically lived at home, he spent most of his time at his girlfriend's flat. Alice was a skinny, vacant watcher of cartoons who had worked as a barmaid in one of Dean's favoured clubs until she tripped over an abandoned crate of WKD and smashed her knee on the stockroom steps. She was not normally perspicacious, but the pain of her ruined patella and ruptured tendons had inspired her to take some photographs as she lay prone on the beery floor. She maintained she'd had no intention of using the photographs for anything, even when Dean approached a no-win no-fee outfit on her behalf; she protested repeatedly that she couldn't possibly sue the club, it was just an accident, poor Gary, what would he do? But she never actually prevented Dean from progressing the claim.

Claire had visited once and found Alice laid out on a stained suedette corner sofa, her splinted knee on a pillow, with one tortoiseshell guinea pig squeaking in her lap and another making a nest behind the TV. An endless parade of *Simpsons* reruns blared across the screen. Dean was poring over paperwork at the table in the corner, galvanised to an intensity of application Claire had never seen in him before by the prospect of his girlfriend possessing a lump sum to disburse.

'Here,' Alice said, thrusting the guinea pig towards him, one hand in its armpits, one cupping its rounded bum. 'Have Mrs Parker. She'll help you fill in the forms.'

'She weed on me last time.'

'She was excited! Here she comes ...'

Alice struggled up from the sofa and limped across the room on her bad leg. She pushed the guinea pig into Dean's face, and he jerked away, tipping back his chair, so that Alice said, 'Oh, you'll hurt her feelings!' She plopped the guinea pig's quivering weight into his arms instead, and Claire watched him accept it, letting it dig its scaly pink feet and transparent claws into the weft of his shirt.

Then there was the Beuys installation at the Pompidou, into which she had stumbled unprepared while her erstwhile friends went in search of Matisse. *Plight*, it was called: two long, low rooms constructed from thick rolls of army-grey felt stacked vertically against one another, some bent and fraying apart, showing their soft stuff. She'd leaned across the plexiglass barrier and taken a breath and felt how the fluff had dried the air. It tickled; it made her cough, but the cough came strangely, as if she had not even opened her mouth, then vanished altogether. A grand piano, shut, stood on the parquet floor, and the very idea of its being played was lost before it could reach her or anyone else, absorbed by the depleted sensorium, in which she had cupped her hands around her ears, buffering herself from the obstinate insistence of a silence not her own.

Strange that Claire had fixated on Callum's death wish, when it was Dean who'd actually tried it: nine paracetamol at the age of fifteen, swallowed dry in bewildered despair, then confessed as soon as his mother returned from the hospice. She had driven him to casualty. Too late for pumping his stomach, the nurses said, but not to worry: nine tablets wasn't likely to do real damage. 'That was what I thought,' she'd said to Claire later on; perhaps to the nurses as well. Saving face. It would have been a professional humiliation to arrive with her own son like that, frantic and furious, on the wrong side of the doors.

They'd made him eat charcoal and kept him two more hours for observation. Then their mother had brought him home again, and parked him in the living room, where Claire and Callum and their father were watching *Goldeneye* on ITV, shifting nervously when the ads came on. Dean sank into an armchair and followed suit. Their mother went straight to the kitchen; then she stomped back down the hall and put her head around the door.

'I suppose I'll make dinner,' she said, 'since none of you have done it in my absence.'

They hadn't, though Claire had popped some popcorn, feeling faintly that this was inappropriate but wanting it all the same. Now it was after ten. The sound of pans banging mingled with the gunfire on TV. Her mother called them through before the film ended, and they ate together at the kitchen table, not mentioning what had happened, but passing the bowl of flabby broccoli from hand to hand with a new, embarrassed solicitude that would not last the week.

It was selfishness that saved him — would go on saving him, Claire thought. The attempt had been, not a cry for help, but a grab for emotional resources, which, once claimed, had provided Dean with all the leverage he needed to abdicate and not be gainsaid. His attempt in some ways had released him; but it had been an especially dangerous moment for Callum, who must have felt the dome around himself finally unseal, lift up, and settle on his younger brother, and mistakenly thought this meant that he, Callum, was now all right — as if the parcel of misery could only belong to one of their parents' children at once, and they'd passed it between them, hand to hand, until the music stopped.

When the doorbell rang, an electronic bing-bong, and Callum jumped up to answer it, wanting, Claire supposed, not to waste the postman's time, her relief seemed to coagulate in the jam jars and the smear of butter on Callum's knife. She wouldn't mention his plight now, then. Maybe later. She got up from the table and went into the living room, where the long curtains that had been closed last night revealed French windows leading out into a square of garden, half gravel, half grass, with one tree — was it a damson tree? — erupting from the lawn, mature enough to be bobbled with green fruit.

The gravel was sharp. The soft, cool grass tore in the grip of her toes. She went towards the tree, because where else was there to go? This was the centrepiece; the only thing with gravitational pull. Reaching it, touching the pewter trunk and gazing up through the net of branches, she saw a bird perched on its highest branch: claws latched, barred wings folded, the yellow thorn of its beak impossibly bright, obviously fake – though that had not prevented her heart from leaping when she spotted it above her, leaping and swelling, as it always used to do when she gazed at the ones at home. A housewarming gift, she immediately thought. Her mother's envoy, sent on ahead to prepare the ground.

She heard Callum crunching over the gravel towards her. She didn't turn around; she wanted first to arrange her face into an expression of withering irony. But the voice that said, 'Claire?' was not Callum's. She spun in fright. Her mother was there: an apparition in a pale linen blouse and blue slacks and Clarks sandals. Claire could not understand how white her mother's eyebrows had become; she could not at first respond, but looked past her mother's expression of practised consternation to where Callum hung back in the doorway, arms folded, frowning the way she'd imagined he would frown when he saw the disastrous flaws in his karyograms: with faint distaste, and total resignation.

'Don't be cross with him,' her mother said. 'He was worried about you.'

'About *me*?'

'He said you showed up very late last night. You'd been drinking. He didn't know what was wrong.' She was looking at Claire with her steady, watery eyes, in the way that Claire remembered and could not stand: as if she was going to hypnotise her and then get her to perform all kinds of humiliating tricks. 'He said you were looking very thin.'

It was hilarious – but also, suddenly, typical, so typical that she should have seen it coming – that Callum would have decided to worry about her. Of course. Only distress could make you move away from Leeds and not come home every single weekend. Only distress could make you do something spontaneous, like having a drink and getting on a train you hadn't booked three months in advance, when the fares were cheapest.

Her mother was holding Claire's shoes. 'Come inside,' she said, and only then did she break eye contact to survey the neighbouring gardens. 'Come and have some breakfast. You didn't eat your toast.'

So he'd told her that as well. When, exactly, had he orchestrated this ambush? First thing, of course. A clandestine phone call before Claire was even awake. All he would've needed to say was, 'Um ... Claire's here,' mild puzzlement badly covered over with polite gladness, and her mother would've been away. *What do you mean, she's there? There in your house? Has something happened?*

He mother was still watching her, awaiting a response. Claire reached up and touched a branch and called to Callum, 'What sort of tree is this?'

The same annoyance that had disfigured Callum's face earlier on now disfigured, momentarily, her mother's. The purple pouches under her eyes seemed to darken, as if the fluid inside them were changing colour in response to her mood. Claire remembered this, too: the torn, the wind-driven sky of her mother's countenance, which set them all, the children, their father as well, furiously winding back whatever it was they'd just said, gathering it in, absorbing it again. Claire's father apparently had not accompanied her mother on this visit. Claire took that as a gesture of solidarity; she imagined him sitting on the bench in the garden, his eyes closed to the sun, saying, 'Just leave the girl alone.'

Her mother turned to look at Callum, giving him permission to answer.

'It's a damson tree,' he dutifully said.

Once the felt's been matted together, it has to be scoured and stretched. You scour with urine, or fuller's earth, or a solution of more soap, submerging the felt and trampling it to release the oils and dirt that have accumulated in the process. It feels counter-intuitive, to dirty something in order to make it clean, but you have to. You have to keep faith with the work.

Callum was fidgeting openly in the doorway. His hands fanned out from his thighs, the fingers spreading and curling in arrhythmic agitation. He was meant to be somewhere else, but couldn't bring himself to announce it. Exits had always been difficult for him. He'd stand like a beaten carthorse for hours, radiating misery, rather than take the blame for ending an encounter. Sometimes Claire had caught him looking on with baffled envy when Dean simply rose from his chair, mid-conversation, and left the room.

It was the hospital, of course: Callum was meant to have left by now, but he'd waited for their mother to arrive and assume responsibility for the situation. For Claire. It was a chain of custody. The overly solicitous breakfast had been designed to keep her put.

'You're going to be late,' Claire said to Callum, over her mother's head. Rubbing it in. Then, to her mother, she said, 'Tell him he can go.'

Callum frowned again, his mouth opening slightly, as if he were going to speak.

'He doesn't need my permission,' her mother said. 'This is his house.'

'Is it? Then why's it full of your things?'

'He bought this house with his own money. He wouldn't take a penny from us, not even for the deposit, would you?'

'He didn't need to. He lived at home that whole time for free.'

Callum seemed finally to accept that his honour was being impugned. 'Look, I don't think,' he began, frowning; but his mother was speaking again.

'Actually not for free. He paid rent. You insisted on paying rent, didn't you?'

Under her fond expectant glare, Callum made a curious gesture, half shrug, half shudder, that seemed to Claire the soul of abjection.

'How *much* did you pay?' she asked.

This time the silence waited for him. He frowned again, slowly. 'That isn't really your—'

'I think they let you pay a couple of hundred a month: more than Dean, who they probably charged nothing, so you'd know you were contributing more than him, but nowhere near what you'd have to pay in your own flat.'

'Even if that *was* the arrangement,' her mother said, 'what's wrong with that? Are you feeling hard done by?'

Of course it would sound that way. How could Claire describe the kinds of dependencies her mother had fostered – the one profoundly emotional, with a veneer of economic self-reliance; the other financial, practical, but emotionally null and void – without sounding like exactly what she was: the middle child, observant, too much left to her own devices, overlooked and disinherited on both sides? How could she explain that sparing Claire the worst of her attentions was the one true gift her mother had had to give?

'I just – *look* at him,' she said in despair, flinging a hand towards her brother. 'Can't you see how miserable he is?'

To which the pair of them responded with identical expressions of exaggerated disbelief that produced in them both the same firm rounded double chin.

'I'm not,' Callum said, meaning *I'm not miserable*, but unwilling to say the word.

'You are. We all are. All three of us. It's not a coincidence. She's got three sad children.'

'Dean's not *sad*,' her mother said.

'He tried to kill himself!'

She looked bewildered. 'He what? He never did that.' Then she feigned realisation – 'You mean the thing in the holidays?' – and made an airy, wafting, dismissive gesture.

'But that was years ago. He was just being silly about a girl. He's fine now.'

'Fine? No job? Staying out all night? Taking drugs?'

'No-o,' she said, with emphasis. 'Didn't he tell you? He's going to university in the autumn. He got his place. He's going to York.'

'St John,' Callum added.

'Yes, that's right. York St John.'

Claire's gaze slid sideways and landed on the gravel. Where the shadow of the house lay across them, the chips of stone looked flat and dull, a uniform charcoal colour; but out of that shadow, in direct sun, they showed beautiful variegations of dove and slate and lilac, not only between separate chips, but within the individual chips themselves. Each glistened with the composite texture of millions of years of relentless compression.

She could feel her mother watching her, hungry for a reaction to the news. But Dean's change of heart about university was not a sign of genuine independence. It wasn't even a bid for his father's approval. It was just a response to what Claire had done – had failed to do – when the department refused her dissertation. Impossible to mark, they said. Not scholarly. A piece of creative writing. Rather wonderful, in its way very captivating, but not what they needed to satisfy the requirements of the degree. She shouldn't worry, though. She could rewrite and resubmit. She'd probably still get a 2:1. This – the lack of consequence, the toothlessness of academe – as much as her pig-headed pride in what she'd written, made her baulk. No, she'd said.

There ought to be a place for creative criticism. If not, the degree was meaningless.

They reasoned with her. They gave her months of grace. They said if only she'd told them in advance what she was doing, they could have helped; but now they'd raised the red flag they couldn't put it down. The more they told her this – the more they emphasised the bureaucratic nature of the obstacle – the more stubborn she became, at first replying to their emails in high dudgeon, then slowly, slowly, as the line didn't change, easing herself away, checking her messages less and less often, throwing herself into life at the bar, where she listened closely when the townies critiqued the weak grasp students had on the hard real world.

And Dean, whom she hardly thought about, had received the whole drama third-hand from Callum, if not second-hand from his mother, and seen a brightness opening in the dark sky of his alienation; though he would not have thought about it quite like that. He would believe he'd arrived independently at the decision to break strike.

'I can't believe he didn't tell you,' Claire's mother said. 'But then ...' – and here she made another face that said *what did you expect?* – 'you haven't been in touch for quite a while.'

'Which makes sense,' Callum said, cautiously. 'If you're saying *you've* been sad.'

It was a pincer movement: she felt them both advance upon her psychically, lowering their spears, holding up nets. Her studied absence, her determination to make it on her own in Manchester, which she had transmitted to them as a signal of her strength, had not been received that way at all; had been scrambled past comprehension when it reached them, transmuted to a cry of pain. They were going to recast her in the family myth.

And this must be – of course it must – the reason why her father hadn't come to the house: not because he thought Claire ought to be left in peace, but because he considered his children's emotional lives the remit of his wife, by virtue of the fact that his wife had attended more deathbeds than he could imagine.

Deathbeds was right, Claire thought. End-of-life care; terminal care; delicate duties of amelioration, and never a need to shake or discomfit, since nothing was going to change. Same here. Callum was, in a sense, already dead; or, he had never become a person, had never grasped the principle of agency, and so could never die; or, his whole life was a deathbed scene, at the end of which he would succumb with perfect resignation, never having done a thing to regret.

She looked up, expecting him to seem ghostly all of a sudden, hovering in the doorway, washed out by the watery morning sun – but he was already gone.

'He's late for work,' her mother said, as if Claire hadn't already noticed and said as much. She was using her clinical, careful tone, slipped on like a pair of gloves, meant to insulate them both from what was really going on. And this was what Claire remembered: always being handled by her mother like this, with a slick, inhuman grasp, as if Claire had been one of those poor kids with desperately compromised immune systems who spend their last days in a plastic tent screaming for a cuddle; as if her mother had known her own touch was the touch of death.

It's a utility. It can be a glass polisher, a shock absorber, a fuel oil filter. It can make tents and hats and shin pads and washers and bumpers and beaters. Dentists use it. Saddlers use it. Silversmiths and cabinet-makers. Military engineers. It can line car boots and coffins. It can *be* a coffin: sustainably produced, biodegradable, tasteful felt shrouds are available from a number of independent felters and funeral homes. Lay your loved one to rest in three layers of heavy-duty British wool felt decorated with the native species of your choice. Let them soak into the fabric, its ultimate fulling.

She slid down the trunk of the damson tree until she was sitting on the grass. Her bare feet stuck out in front of her, bigger than the stone urn thriving with mint that her mother had now begun to weed as if it were hers. It basically was. One day, Claire thought, one day my father will be dead, he'll die first, and my mother will come to live in this house with Callum, and that will be what they both want, in their understanding of 'want'. Dean will sneer at them, but he'll rely on Callum to do the caring; he'll only visit every couple of months, when she's all clean and propped up in her chair, and he won't chip in unless he's asked. Years hence.

And Claire – where would she be? She tried to picture herself in this scene: she tried to imagine making tea while her mother held court with a tartan rug across her knees, and Dean dropped the news that at the age of forty-six he had finally fathered a child. But she couldn't do it. She wasn't there, or anywhere else. It frightened her that she could see their futures so clearly but could not catch a glimpse of her own. Something was there, waiting for her, beyond the shut piano, in the second room you were not allowed to enter but could only imagine. Whatever it was, was it waiting for her to create it? Or waiting for her to kid herself she had? After all, Dean thought he was the engineer of his own identity. Callum thought he'd turned his back on social convention. What was Claire deluding herself about?

She knew what her mother would say to that – though she'd never use the word 'deluding'. She'd say that Claire had got the wrong idea about her family. They weren't dysfunctional. They were ordinary, with an ordinary share of problems, an ordinary share of love. Claire gripped two fistfuls of grass. What if she *was* the one in trouble? Her brothers were resigned to their lots, and she'd always identified that as the source of their vulnerability; but maybe it was *lack* of resignation that left you exposed – that gave you this feeling of something vast perpetually being at stake. Callum had never entertained the possibility of existence being other than it was. Dean had never thought beyond simple negation. But Claire had been host and prey to both of those ideas. She was out in Manchester trying to prove them.

Except she wasn't out in Manchester, was she? She was here. This was the danger: wanting to be both at once. Those were the plates moving apart, the gap she could plummet down. She half-expected the earth to start quaking, to split around the root of the damson tree and show her the dark earth, the torn and dangling worms, all the coffins smashed and leaking and the mantle boiling through ... But the ground was steady, and the grass beneath the tree was tough and scratchy with thistle. The seat of her jeans clung to it: it wouldn't let her slump to the ground. She remembered how Callum's felted figurines had clung to the hillsides they stood upon, the minute resistance she'd felt as she pulled one away, the almost imperceptible sound of fibres tearing – though if you turned the figure over and examined its base, you'd see no obvious damage.

As you work it, the felt shrinks. Its edges turn wavy, ragged; it ripples and the dips fill up with foam. You think it's ruined, and sometimes it is; but sometimes it's only approaching its new form. You pour on more water to rinse the fulling suds away, and then, when it's relatively clean, you stretch it out to dry on a great frame called a tenter, from which we get the phrase 'to be on tenterhooks', meaning 'to be suspended'.

NO TWO WERE E'ER WED

He had to get down and lift the flounced valance and push his hand between the mattress and the boxspring, groping around, his wrist compressed. There was nothing – then a corner. An edge. He pinched and dragged it out. It was not quite as blue as he remembered. The elasticated strap around its middle stood out brightly, but the cloth binding was muted, greyish, the texture faintly ridged. The scarlet ribbon poking from the shut pages was forked at the end like a tongue.

Somehow David had known Claire would not have taken the notebook to her Spanish lesson. You don't sling your fetish object in a rucksack under a table to get kicked all night: you keep it somewhere safe. How hard could it be to find? But once he'd searched the bedside table drawers, turning up only her gelatinous purple vibrator, dull with dust, and her Nancy Friday paperback of women's fantasies, and then discovered, down the back of the desk, a splayed copy of Hume's *On*

Suicide, he had begun to realise how mysterious the bedroom was. New hiding places kept occurring to him as he sat on the bed and looked around. Was it buried in the laundry basket? Behind the storage heater? Taped to the back of the mirror? Even once he'd hit on the space beneath the mattress, other possibilities kept occurring to him. There might be a horde of notebooks surrounding him even now.

He pulled gently on the little red ribbon. Had the notebook been a gift from this new friend Claire had made, this Caro (never Caroline), with whom she kept going out for sushi and pad thai at the pan-Asian restaurant on South Street? Caro was a queer theorist – perhaps the first queer theorist ever to work at the university. She came from Whitechapel. She had wide, staring eyes, and when David first met her she had stared at him as no woman had stared at him before, completely without sexual interest but rather with horrified curiosity, the same way you might study a monstrously large spider before you took the nozzle of the vacuum cleaner to it. He could picture Caro as a notebook-keeper, furiously recording every passing judgement about her new place of work and the people in it. Had Claire met Caro in London, they would not have become friends. He had seen Claire in London: she was the proverbial country mouse, trembling in the cavern of King's Cross. This place suited her better. She could walk the full span, from the bus station to the ruins, in less than ten minutes, and feel she knew it all. But Caro, he could see, was already pining for the city. She was already wondering what on Earth she had done. For years now David had watched the influx and retreat of members of staff across the Faculty of Arts and Humanities, the bright young things who came north with their four-star-potential research portfolios to put in a respectable couple of years before they fled back to the golden triangle of Oxbridge and UCL. Caro was one of them. The nature reserves along the coast, the rubbery seals basking on sandbars, the dark sky protection that rendered the weaker constellations visible, meant nothing to her. She was horrified by the stale Guinness in the Lachlan Hotel bar, the family-friendly musicals at the Roscoe Theatre. She wore her fake fur coat at all times, as if she was afraid that taking it off would signal belonging.

Even worse was Caro's effect on Claire's research. The monograph was so close to completion now, and so dreadfully overdue, that sometimes, when David caught Claire watching *Grey's Anatomy* on Netflix, he wanted to shake her. Couldn't she see it was nearly done? That the press, the department, wouldn't wait for ever? Nobody took this long to convert their thesis into a monograph. If she didn't get it out in time for the REF, she'd be moved to a teaching-only contract: the death knell of research careers. These long lunches with Caro, the drinks after teaching, were further distractions. Even worse, Caro's endless patter about hybridity and intersectionality and fluid gendering and whatever else was making Claire ashamed of her project, which seemed stolid and old-fashioned by comparison. She had become prone to fits of despair in which she threatened not to finish at all, to mothball the book and start something else more cutting-edge.

'Don't be stupid,' he would say. 'You're being cutting-edge about Lady Mary Shepherd. Nobody's written about her before.'

'But that's exactly the problem,' Claire would protest. 'Why am I writing about someone that nobody else is interested in?'

'What do you think 'cutting edge' *means*?'

Eventually he would be able to console her. Sniffling, she would get back to work. But for how long? Soon there would be another bento box with Caro. More talk of collaborative installations. He wished Claire were not so credulous. More robust. At the same time, though, didn't he wish she were readier to take impressions from *him*? Everyone thought she was so timid – so sweet. Only he seemed to know about the rank stubbornness that ran through her like the wire in a twisty tag; how, despite her professed reservations about the book, she fought him bitterly on every point he dared to question; on the very urgency of finishing it at all.

He liked to think he was attracted to a certain academic ferocity in a woman, a hard-won independence. He had male colleagues who wanted, pathologically needed, to mould their partners' intellects after their own, but he wasn't like that. And if his and Claire's disagreements had been scholarly in the main, he felt sure that they would have been all right. But many other battlegrounds erupted too, as if to force him into this posture he wanted to reject. If he said, very delicately, that Claire's jumper was shapeless and unflattering, then she would deliberately keep wearing it, punishing him for having the temerity to comment on her clothes – as if he was some rank–and–file overbearing boyfriend, not an ally trying to protect her from the consequences of her low self-esteem. She had a small tattoo of a unicorn on her ankle, which she went to great lengths to cover in the summer, but which she would not consider, not for a second, getting removed. And she neglected her personal hygiene. She'd go three, four days without having a shower, until he was forced to round on her and say, 'Can't you smell yourself? Can't you take responsibility for your own body?' It was maddening. She laid herself wide open to someone like Caro, inadvisedly, confusingly open; and yet she was completely closed to all benevolent influence from him, her partner, who loved her, who had her best interests at heart.

The showering, he'd noticed, had improved since Caro arrived. Every time Claire set off for one of those lunches, her hair was fluffy, freshly washed. Her nails were trimmed. He ought to have been glad of this: he was always hoping she would spruce herself up. But then he would watch her choose one of those mannish shirts she had started buying, white twill or grey denim, watch her button it up to the neck, and feel uneasy. It wasn't even that Claire was copying Caro's style, with her fake fur and her blue tights, but rather that Claire was dressing how she imagined Caro might *want* her to: complementing rather than competing. Was there something flirtatious in it? Not that he thought Claire and Caro were sleeping together – but he wondered if Claire had thought about it. Caro would have. Why not? Here she was, hundreds of miles from home, the new face in her department, single, and by her own admission 'sexually rapacious'. Who else was she going to audition? To seduce? Claire was beautiful to David, an Augustan plaster cameo – dark hair against a pale, high forehead; delicate eyebrows with a distinctive semicircular shape; deep-set eyes; the strong, steep slope of her nose – but she could also be beautiful to others, if she let it show. Was that what she thought she was doing?

When they had first compared their sexual histories, David had told Claire, truthfully, that he'd slept with a grand total of six girls, and she had said, 'Me too,' and in his relief he'd made an awkward joke about not knowing that Claire liked girls. He often remembered that moment: his foolish acceptance of the matching number, but also the joke. Had he hit on the truth by accident? Was Claire really interested in women? She had never expressed any curiosity to him; and here she was, living with a man, calling herself his girlfriend. He had to respect the identity she chose to assert. Who wants to be the idiot who decides his lover is gay just because she doesn't want to sleep with him any more? But even with all the respecting he had done, even with all the work, their sex life was still a disaster. He believed, profoundly believed, that she was just as frustrated as him, but didn't know it. What else might she not know about herself?

He opened the notebook at random and started to read.

G. was a comedian, or wanted to be. We were both very drunk when we met for the first time in the union and went back to his room. He told me later that he'd already vomited and then continued drinking before we even spoke to each other. I said that was disgusting, and he immediately said that I'd stunk of garlic because

I'd been for Chinese with my friends, so we were even. He was very skinny: I must have weighed more than him. We fucked in his narrow single bed, me on top, so hammered our carelessness extended to the sex itself, which we never really finished. We saw each other a handful of times, always with mutual friends, and always ending up in bed, despite the fact that we seemed to hate one another, to have skipped straight to the bitterness of the soon-to-be-no-more. The night he left the union leading a different girl by the hand, right past me, right in front of me, I cried on the shoulder of someone I wanted to call my friend, not because I was surprised, but because I had known it was coming and been unable to stop myself.

Carelessness! David and Claire's intimacies were now so few and far between that each separate event was etched on him as deeply as an injury: he could at any given moment remember the last time he had seen his girlfriend's pale, mole-dotted breasts, or touched the softness of her sex. Now, for example, as he knelt beside the bed with the notebook in his hands, he knew absolutely that the last time they made love had been in the Christmas holidays, when they both returned from their respective family visits suffused with the relief that, however much they disappointed one another, at least they weren't bound by blood. Their arrangements were elective, and in that new appreciation of choice they had gone almost merrily to bed together. He came desperately, triumphantly, and as they collapsed against each other in the high bed he'd trembled with surging healthiness, a sense of having been restored, and a painful, tender hope that perhaps, this time, they might have turned a corner. The feeling had been so strong that he'd let himself get carried away. Huddled under the duvet, in the nest of warmth their efforts had made, he'd said, without thinking, 'Doesn't this feel good? Don't you feel better? I feel so much better', and instantly she had tensed against him, her back locking up, as if he'd said, 'See? I told you so!'

That had been on December the twenty-eighth. Now it was the twenty-first of February. Nothing had changed how he wanted it to change, though he could not say it hadn't changed at all. She wouldn't talk about it. She seemed to want to claim that she had nothing to say; but the problem was itself evidence of a powerful and complicated inner life, one on which he had little purchase, but which he could not help suspecting was somehow within reach. She teased him with it: teased him with the evidence and never the explanation. Of course she said things – she knew she couldn't get away with saying nothing – but what she said was always beside the point. She would tell him she didn't *not* want sex, she just didn't want it as often as him. She would say that sex was very mental for her, which meant that when she was deep in her research she had no resources to spare. She would say it was emotional, too. If she and David were not communicating well, if she didn't feel close to him, then it became impossible for her to venture safely into those turbulent affective waters.

During such exchanges, he felt bound to point out to her that if they were not communicating well it was because Claire was refusing to engage in communication. She was talking calmly, even plausibly, and to an outsider this would

all sound reasonable, but not to David. He knew, with absolute certainty, that what she was saying was a dodge, and he
felt insulted, and told her so. How could she present this stuff
about sex being mental and emotional as if she were unusual
in that – as if sex were not mental and emotional for him?
Did she think he was a robot? A dog?

At some point during this conversation, she would have
begun to cry. Her cheeks wet, almost chafed-looking, she
would tell him that the birth control pills and the antidepressants she was taking had suppressed her libido and made her
breasts sore and caused her to gain weight (not true, in David's
eyes), which made her body feel alien to her, and exacerbated
the anxiety she already felt about her nakedness. And, she
would add, there was also the basic problem of the flat being
cold and damp. She knew he didn't think it was important,
but it was to her. No matter how long the storage heaters had
been running, as soon as her skin was exposed to the air it
broke out in goosebumps that rendered her unable to appreciate other sensations. All she wanted was to dress herself again.

'I'm sorry,' she would weep. 'I'm not giving you what you
want. My body just won't co-operate.'

How could he argue with this? He was not a chauvinist.
He understood that his partner was not at his beck and call;
that the world placed enough pressure on Claire's flesh already
without him adding to it. How could he articulate his deep
conviction – that she would be happier if she addressed her
issues with sex – without sounding as if he was manipulating
her into meeting his needs by presenting them as her own?
So he released the pressure: he put his arms around her and

said, 'Come on, I love you, please stop crying, please don't be upset,' and things like that.

It was a good thing, then, it had to be a good thing, that she was allowing herself to write in this notebook, diary, whatever it was, about sex; but David noticed, and was amused by, his disappointment that the passage was not about him. Had he come to the notebook only to look for himself, not for Claire? And yet his neck was burning, as if he had been exposed somehow, as if he and this character G. – whom he'd never heard about before – were not entirely separate men. He too had been drawn into the boisterous drinking of male students, had been sick and then drunk water and then kept going, down the glittering streets towards the girls; but he would not have told the girls about it, not even later on. He would have been ashamed. That was what you got for sleeping with someone who fancied themselves a comedian: the amount of self-loathing they felt would always dwarf any loathing they could provoke in others, an imbalance which had few consolations, but did at least leave them free to reveal their most awful indiscretions for effect.

David was aware of something hysterical in his rush to judge this man, a kind of desperate warding-off, but this awareness did not stop his gaze from flinching towards the facing page, where he found another block of text, this time much shorter.

Someone whose name I never found out, who I met in a club xx xxxxx and went home with. He was rolling drunk, and he told me he'd like to 'nail' me, so I let him, and it took him thirty seconds, and that was that.

The word 'nail', scare-quoted like that, stood proud of the text. It was a brutal, a terrible word. He had no doubt it was the right one. He had no doubt that the memories were real. She was getting it all down, the partners she had had before David, more than six of them, many more, who formed what she had described to David, in a wincing, ironic way, as her 'chequered past', after they had been together for more than a year. He had rushed to reassure her that he did not mind: neither the fact of the previous lovers, nor her having lied to him at first. Their relationship had been a succession of lies and revelations of this type. He'd felt like he was getting to know Claire vertically; that he was continually falling through a series of layers, each giving way in staggered succession, like the floors of a fire-gutted building. She had only slept with six people; no, she had slept with dozens. How many? She wasn't sure.

These successive disillusionments did not deliver him anywhere, the great wheel did not revolve, but with every new confession he had a sense of getting closer to what was really there. He was convinced that she'd lied, not from malice, but from fear. She had been afraid of accepting this historical version of herself. David, to his surprise, had found himself equally resistant. He could not accept the updated, the corrected, the 'true' Claire that she was showing to him. Not that he didn't believe that she'd had many partners, many unsuitable ones. He was sure she had. And not that he struggled with it for personal reasons, vain petty jealousies or puritan idealisations. He didn't. What he couldn't accept was her absorption of this history into the depth of her being; the way she allowed it to twist her sense of herself. He believed – he had told her as much – that she had not *been herself* when those things occurred.

For example: she cared about words, their precision. She agonised over sentences. It took her an hour to write a postcard on holiday. When David used a word that offended her – *cunt*, for example – she scowled at him. She distanced herself. She was embarrassed by dirty talk. So how could 'nail' have persuaded her to yield? Only if she wasn't being herself. She would not have known it at the time, but she must know it now. To yield had been an act of self-deceit. Why else, when she wrote in the notebook, had she held the word aloft with quotes, as if with a pair of tongs? They seemed to signal her awareness of the horror of the word, and her need to disown it – to give it back to the man who had given it to her.

Even as he mulled over the nailing, David felt something strenuous and deliberate in his reflections, and knew that he was still distracted by thoughts of himself; by the possibility that Claire could have written about him in this way. Was he really so narcissistic? Was he really just dwelling on the confession Claire had chosen to make, her choice – or rather the man's choice – of words, in order to prove to himself, or to some invisible bank of spectators, that he was not simply rushing through the notebook in search of his own image? Or could some benevolent reason be found for this preoccupation: an eagerness to know how he came across to her, how their life seemed to her, in case there were obvious problems he could address?

He turned to the entries she had written most recently, hoping to discover there something about himself on which he would be able to prove the nobility of his intentions.

When I was seven, me and Diane would go to the girls' toilets at lunchtime and lock ourselves in a stall and rub each other between the legs. Diane had a shaggy fringe that got in her eyes. She wore shoes with little high heels and frilly white ankle socks. She was the initiator. I didn't resist. The guilt was exciting, like getting the giggles at story-time, sitting on the carpet, knowing you ought to shut up. One day a teacher came into the toilets. She banged on the door of the stall and said, 'Hurry up in there!' It scared me and I told Diane I didn't want to do it any more. She pouted. She was stroppy, a bit wild. When my mother collected me that afternoon, Diane ran up to her and shouted, 'Claire's been having SEX!' It was revenge. My mother would have dismissed the accusation if I'd brazened it out. Who would believe something like that of their seven-year-old? But I didn't know that. I was consumed with shame and began to cry. I cried all the way home. In the kitchen I confessed. My mother pursed her lips. She said, Diane's a dirty girl.

Had he been exploring at the age of seven? He didn't think so. Not with other kids, at least. Surely there had been sexual thoughts, absurd stirrings caused by the female characters in cartoons: Jessica Rabbit, that sort of thing. But nothing as *active* as the events Claire described: the dirty girl (what had become of her?), the toilet stalls, Claire's disapproving mother. He could picture the latter scene with lurid clarity

– the long kitchen in the house where Claire's parents still lived, the oilcloth-covered table, the heavy television that must have been ancient even then, with Claire's childish, tear-stained face reflected in the bulging screen. He could see her mother wearing one of those ugly waxed aprons, too. Everything wipeable.

Suddenly he thought of the rippling walls of the Wendy house in Lars's back garden, Lars of the Swedish mother, who hadn't looked especially Swedish, but had given her slack, wet-looking mouth to her son. They had been out in the garden together, him and Lars and Lars's little sister – he couldn't remember her name – and another girl called Kim. Lars's sister's Wendy house was pitched out there, and she had led them all inside it, where the grass was itchy and damp and the sunshine glowed through the coloured walls and it smelled of warm plastic. She had asked Lars to show them his *thing* again (again!), which he did, pulling the waistband of his shorts away from his belly and letting them look inside, though David didn't look. The girls had laughed; Kim had covered her freckled face. Then Lars's sister had turned to him, to David, and asked him to do the same; and David had felt suddenly suffocated in the hot plastic silence of the little Wendy house with the blue and red patches burning on his face, and without answering, without even thinking, he had pushed past Lars on his hands and knees, through the hanging flap that was printed to look like a door, out, out, into the fresh air, with the girls' mocking laughter behind him.

He was running out of time. Spanish would have finished already; Claire would be walking home. He turned the pages backwards, scanning for D.s, and saw none. When he reached the beginning, he read the first entry in the book.

M. took my virginity in a Novotel. He had a settlement because of his injury and he spent it on things like that – hotel rooms for us, meals, cinema tickets. He loved me. I loved him. We used to order room service – I had no idea of the cost, and he never said. I was seventeen and we had been seeing each other for two months. He was twenty-three, tall and slim, with a long, slender penis I'd already touched. He knew this was my first time and he was very patient, very concerned. He would have stopped instantly if I'd asked him to. I didn't, though. I was nervous but I wanted to go ahead. I felt safe with him. The heavy curtains were drawn, it was very dusky in the room. I remember the snapping sound as he put the condom on. He didn't want me to help him with it, though I had been expecting to – Cosmopolitan always seemed to be full of advice about how to put a condom on your man, with your mouth, even. He lowered himself on to me. Intercourse was faintly painful and faintly nice. He came, but he was holding back, so it was muted. I didn't. I didn't even think about faking. I didn't bleed, either, and that disappointed me. There should have been a sign that something had changed.

Had Claire ever faked with *him*? He recoiled from the idea. It was a joke, the faked female orgasm; something from lazy comedies, an attack on the sexual pride of arrogant men. He didn't make assumptions about Claire's pleasure. He'd given her every opportunity to tell him what she liked, to slow things down. Of course some women faked it – what was to stop them? But these were women with boorish husbands, or women who were incapable of climaxing at all. Claire wasn't one of *them*. And he'd be able to tell, wouldn't he? He'd be able to tell if the noises were not convincing. The relaxation of her body, the clenching spasms, even the smell that came off her afterwards, a mineral sort of smell, as if some heavy metal had been expelled – that couldn't be faked, could it?

He read the entry again, forcing himself to concentrate on its larger significance. As first times went, it didn't sound bad. There had been love in the room. Generosity. A neutral space, not her childhood bedroom, not his flat. Presumably Claire had fallen asleep beside M. that night. He felt glad for her, straightforwardly, not jealously, glad. And yet the dominant mood in the writing was one of disappointment: about the lack of bleeding, the faintness of sensation, none of it enough to make the night count as an event. And was there a further disappointment, even beyond this – that M. had been kind and considerate, had held himself back and not been over-come with passionate excitement? But that was what came of losing your virginity to someone so much older than yourself – someone who knew what they were getting themselves into. A boy of Claire's own age would never have been that careful and in control. David thought of his own first time, with Lindsay, his first real girlfriend, when they were both eighteen. They'd done it in his bedroom when his parents were out for the afternoon. He'd put a towel down on the bed, and thank God he did, because Lindsay bled so much they had to stop: not at her behest – she would have kept going – but at his. The sight of blood on his penis as he thrust in and out had made him feel sick. Made him soft. They tried again the following weekend, and this time they saw it through, but she dumped him two weeks later, in the Odeon foyer, after he had queued up and bought her a Pepsi and a chocolate Häagen-Dazs. She made him stand there holding them, the Häagen-Dazs melting down his hand, while she explained in an almost angry way that he was too intense. She didn't like all the mix-tapes he made for her, the way he followed her around. He remembered how her braces had glinted in the harsh overhead lights; his groaning disappointment that she would not still be his girlfriend when the braces came off.

In the days that followed his first glimpse of the notebook's contents, David tried to track what conversations, what triggers, might eventually find their way into the things Claire wrote. The notebook was there in his mind every day, as it must have been in hers. At night, lying in bed, he seemed to sense it far beneath him, a ridge in his back, like the pea in the fairy tale; he almost wanted to turn to her and say, 'Can you feel something?'

He tried to provoke her into writing about him. He wasn't proud of it, but there it was. He tried to take her to bed. Reading the diary had suffused him with a stupid, blind hopefulness that maybe now he possessed the insight that would allow him to solve their problems. So he put his arms around her one evening when she was frying onions, a sort of bear hug from behind, which she liked him to do; but then the warmth of her back, her soft waist, made him hard, and he allowed himself to press against her.

'Don't,' she said. 'They'll burn.'

'Take them off the heat.'

'You want me to stop cooking?'

'I want *you*.'

That had confused her. Usually his pride would have made him withdraw after the comment about burning the onions. They had a dance, and those were the steps. He made an overture. She said something deliberately unsexy. He recoiled. But this time he'd persisted. He'd been direct. She wasn't prepared for that. She went quiet, and he didn't realise she was crying, not at first, because he was still standing behind her: he thought maybe she was warming up to the idea. But then he felt the tears dropping on his hands where he'd clasped them around her waist.

'Don't,' he'd said, dragging her around to face him. 'Look at me. Stop crying. It's just another dodge.'

'It's not a dodge!' She was angry now. She was still holding the spatula coated with onion grease. 'I can't help it.'

'How do you know? You never even try.'

'I do try! You think I *want* to be crying?'

'Yeah,' he said, 'I do.'

She shoved the spatula against him, smearing his shirt, and fled the room. Her sobs increased in volume as the distance between them expanded. The bedroom door slammed.

How could this not make it into the notebook? But when he next had a chance to look, on Claire's heavy teaching afternoon, he found a single new block of text.

K. was a steroid abuser with bulging veins in his neck. He showed me the steroids, little ampules and syringes that arrived in un-

marked packages from Eastern Europe. He said you had to be careful not to do too much or your dick would shrink. We went to a loud bar where he shouted over the music. I don't remember what he was shouting about except for two things. The first thing was that his ex-girlfriend had been a snowboarder and they used to use her snowboard to hold her legs apart during sex. She would put the boots on and step into the bindings and lie there wearing the snowboard like a spreader-bar. The second thing was that one summer he worked on a building site alongside illegal Ukrainian immigrants. The Ukrainians went on strike when their pay was held up for several weeks, and then they blamed the foreman, and hanged him from a scaffold. I was on my period, which was the excuse I gave for not wanting to fuck when we got back to his flat, but that wasn't the main reason. I was in the middle of my genital wart infection, and I had a cluster of warts at the entrance to my vagina. I didn't tell him this. I just blamed my period. I wouldn't even take my knickers off. Nevertheless he got hold of the string of my tampon and tugged it a little bit. He said he found that exciting – having the power to pull it out. I liked it too, so he kept tugging on the string while I stroked my clit. No doubt if we'd had full sex I would never have come, but I came like that, horribly ashamed of myself, disgusted, but excited nonetheless.

David knew about the STD – one of her revelations, after they'd already slept together – but he did not want to imagine the 'cluster' (what a word!). He had never seen the warts himself. They had been treated, removed, whatever, before he and Claire got together. Her skin didn't seem to be scarred or marked in any way. Reading this now, he saw how easily it could have been worse. The guy was shooting up, for God's sake, with unmarked needles that came in the post. He might have had HIV. How could David *not* feel censorious about this? Or about Claire exposing someone to a virus without their consent? She ought to have declared what she had. Had she declared everything to *him*? He gave a sort of fascinated shudder at the remote possibility that he might, unbeknownst to himself, and surely unbeknownst to Claire, be infected with something serious – though he had no symptoms to speak of, and they would have announced themselves by now, after five years together, wouldn't they? He found he was soothed enough by this logic, and by the firm distinction between himself and this guy, this K., a moron, a muscle-bound freak, to forget the idea. At least Claire had respected David enough to tell him outright.

Nothing about K. and his misdeeds seemed to link to anything Claire had said that week. None of the images connected with images from their lives – he could not read the entry like that, like a dream's juggling of associations; he could not see why this memory, of all possible memories, had floated to the surface of her mind. He could only draw a tenuous and unsatisfying parallel between the physical humiliation of the episode and the psychological humilia-tion both of them had felt in the kitchen when he put his arms around her. This was part of the notebook's general disorganisation. The entries were not set down in any clear chronological order, but jumped from childhood to adult-hood to adolescence. Nor were they arranged by serious-ness. Memories of flings and one-night-stands intercut with long-term relationships; encounters of profound abjection sat alongside moments of surprising tenderness. It annoyed him. Had Claire taken a more logical approach to her records, then the whole thing might have been a useful exercise for her. But was it even written for her? Did anyone in this day and age still keep a private journal they expected never to be found? It was hard to believe in the persistence of genuinely onanistic writing in a society that had so complacently accepted the institution of mass surveillance and the erosion of private space. Wouldn't Claire, no matter what she *thought* she was doing, imagine a reader at all times? And wouldn't that reader, by virtue of circumstance if nothing else, have to be him?

Not all the episodes recorded in the notebook involved a partner.

I was on my break, alone in the staffroom, sitting on one of the low chairs around the coffee table. It entered my head suddenly to touch myself — almost out of boredom; almost because I'd read all the magazines that were lying around. So I slid my hand down the front of my jeans, into my knickers, and I was almost immediately very wet. One of my colleagues could have walked into the room at any time. I thought there was a good chance I'd be able to whip my hand out of my jeans before they saw, but I couldn't be sure. The absolute inappropriateness of what I was doing, the prospect of being caught, was part of the attraction. But nobody walked in, and in the end I came so fast there was still some time to kill, so I picked up one of the magazines anyway, and read an article I'd read before.

The fact of Claire touching herself, voluntarily, alone, was precious to him: it seemed as free of their current problems as anything could be. Nobody was there demanding sex. The desire for a sexual experience had simply risen up of its own accord, despite the obstacles arrayed against it. How rare this seemed to be for her now; how almost unheard of. Her innate sexual urges had become like creatures hunted to the point of extinction. And yet the fact that Claire was writing this note-book at all was reason to be hopeful. Something had spurred her on to begin it. Something had kept her coming back.

David briefly let himself consider the possibility that the notebook was in some sense a rebuke to Claire's mother, who would have found the candour of the writing unbearable. She and Claire were like a bird and its fledgling, except the wrong way around: it was Anne who required that every piece of information she received from her daughter be pre-chewed, denatured, made bland and easily digestible; it was Anne who held her beak open in helplessness for its chasm to be filled. She was morbidly obese, and David had always interpreted Claire's own thinness as a reaction against her mother's soft expansion. The stubbornness – Claire's stubbornness – was her mother's too. Anne possessed the same intractable core. David thought of her fatness as a deliberate self-modification, like Claire's tattoo, except that the tattoo was meant to adver-tise some aspect of Claire's purported self, whereas Anne's size was an act of subterfuge intended to hide what she actually was, to make her seem weak-willed and harmless, even pitiful in certain lights – though pity was an emotion you expressed towards Anne at your peril. He remembered once trying to help her out of the car at the supermarket: the gimlet-eyed rage with which she had regarded his outstretched hand.

At last he discovered a D.

The first time I slept with D. was in a Premier Inn on the out-skirts of York, halfway from him to me. We'd been Skyping each other for weeks, agreeing and refining what we would do when we were finally together. In the hotel room he slapped my breasts, gently at first, then harder when I didn't change my mind. It stung at first, not unpleasantly. Then the slaps became heavier, his hand slamming into the soft breast tissue with dull thuds. My breasts went very red and the nipples were numb with shock. I wanted to please him so perfectly he would leave his wife, so I let him keep going. I asked what else he fantasised about doing, and he said punching me in the stomach. It wasn't the answer I expected. Spanking, choking, yes — but wasn't this too much like two men fighting? I let him do it anyway. I tensed my abs. He pulled his punch, but the breath still barked out of me. I still folded in half. Within an hour, my breasts were covered in blue and purple bruises. I showed them to him, I found it almost funny how bad they looked, and in a second he was hard again.

He read this with heavy recognition. The D. wasn't him, but in their early days together Claire had also tried to convince David that she was a masochist. This had been another of the lies he'd had to fight his way past. In bed together, she writhed against him as if he'd pinned her down. That was the way she operated: not to ask for things she wanted, but to behave as if they had already occurred, leaving him to infer her desires from these incongruous responses to imagined actions on his part, like a *Jeopardy* contestant given the answer first. His inferences were wrong at the beginning. The writhing made him think he'd really hurt her, so he'd stop and pull away, but then Claire would let out a little mew of frustration at this; she'd draw him back towards her, draw his weight down, until at last he understood that she wanted to be crushed: she wanted him to bear down on her, to hold her wrists above her head and kick her feet apart, all mobility and agency lost as he sealed her mouth with an endless kiss. Part of him had been interested, of course. Claire must have known that. She must have sensed in him some latent curiosity about, even capacity for, the ridiculous postures of domination. But this had not made him willing to comply. He'd gone a little way with her – the holding, the crushing, was not so bad – but when she began to encourage him to spank her, presenting her buttocks to him in an embarrassing schoolgirlish way, he'd rejected the whole set-up – the silence in particular, because when you were dealing with questions of consent, someone had to speak.

'No,' he'd said, rolling her off his lap, drawing the covers over himself. 'What you're asking me to do . . .'

'Don't you like it?'

'Maybe. I don't know. It's supposed to be what men want, isn't it? But I've never heard a woman talk convincingly about liking it. It's really hard for me to trust that claim. I mean, it's abuse we're talking about here. Liking being abused – how can that not come from a very bad place?'

He would not participate, he'd said: not on these terms, perhaps not ever. Claire had wept in a wide-eyed disbelieving way, as if he'd said he wanted to see other people, not that he could not bring himself to strike her soft beloved flesh. She insisted that her preferences were her preferences. Whatever she claimed, he ought to believe.

N. took me to a holiday place his parents owned. He got a soft black rope and wound it around my torso in a complicated pattern, binding my breasts so the nipples poked up and began to swell. He told me to kneel down and suck his cock. I did. After a minute, he said, disgustedly, Are you serious? You'll never make me come like that.

Here they were – the men to whom she'd sold this version of herself before she tried selling it to David. The men who had been so willing to respect the labels she self-applied.

Z. lived on the south coast. I had to go through London and out the other side to meet him. He was pale and skinny with a shaved head and lots of piercings, and he was very visible on the scene, with various profiles, a blog, etc., but single for all that. He used the word 'play' as if it were a serious thing. We met at the station, then he walked me back to his flat. We stopped at Iceland along the way to buy frozen pizzas for dinner. I began to look down on him then. At the flat, which was scruffy, like a student house, we baked and ate the pizzas, and he showed me some extreme pornography he liked: a girl getting her labia sewn shut with black thread, six stitches either side, criss-cross like a laced-up shoe, then her lips, then her eyes. The thin skin of her eyelids stretched and stretched on the point of the needle until I thought it would never break through. Afterwards he got me to lie on his orange futon and he gave me a back massage. He said my back was unbelievably tense. The muscles were knotted solid. How can you go around all the time as tense as this? He also said something about the blackheads on my chin, and I said I didn't have blackheads, because I thought blackheads were exactly that — literally big black pinheads that looked as prominent as the studs in his face. But he just prodded my chin and said, no, girl, those are blackheads right there. He meant the little bumps that never went away. Then he put a ball-gag in my mouth, a red ball on a black leather strap, and started to fuck me from behind. He slapped my arse. I felt absolutely nothing. I was dry as a bone. I didn't fancy him. I didn't even like him. The gag made it hard to breathe; it made my jaw ache. I began to cry. He said, Jesus, girl, you know we can stop. We stopped. It wasn't midnight yet. We still had hours to go before I could leave and catch my train. We lay there on his futon in the dark and talked about his loneliness, the kind of girl he wanted. He was angry with me for coming all that way and then not being into him. You knew what I looked like, he said. You knew how skinny I was.

David could not bring himself to contemplate this ghastly individual, this merchant of pain, who was ugly in every conceivable way. Instead he found himself thinking about the logistics of the journey. The south coast: that was a hell of a trek for Claire. Not that she would have set off from Scotland, not back then; but even from Nottingham it was a long way to go, right into London then off the train and across the city to Victoria to catch a second train south. It would have taken hours – the best part of a day. And all that time, she'd been travelling towards *him*: someone so obviously unsuitable for her that David had been able to tell it was a bad idea by the third sentence.

This was one of the things that made him suspicious of so-called subs and doms: that they were not the enlightened beacons of self-awareness, the taboo-breaking pioneers, that they claimed to be, but rather damaged souls who could not connect with one another unless some pre-existing formal arrangement removed the bulk of the negotiation that was usually required. It worried him especially about self-proclaimed submissive women. Trying to untangle his own feelings, after the debacle with Claire, he had gone online, in private mode, and browsed a couple of BDSM connections websites; and he found that these women's profiles, 'sassy' as they might be designed to appear, always seemed to him terribly vulnerable, claiming a wide range of attributes that were simply window-dressing to the fact that they were really trading on their submissiveness as the best quality they had to offer – which, to dominant men, it apparently was.

Such women would have scoffed at David's reservations, of course. They would have said they weren't damaged, they were just bored by vanilla sex, and if more people acknow-ledged their deep sexual boredom as they had done then the world would be a better place. The whole BDSM commu-nity was – it liked to say – 'safe, sane and consensual'. But who exactly was consenting? Was it the submissive woman's real self, or was it — as in Claire's case — a false self she had constructed in order to gain approval from a community that seemed willing to give it to her? Who could tell the difference? Who cared enough to try?

Somebody caned me. I don't remember who, I just remember saying yes, he could do it, when he showed me the cane. Getting on all fours on the bed. The whooshing sound of the cane coming down, then the crack as it hit my arse. The pain lagging behind, so there was a split second in which I thought caning was no big deal. Then a sting — small at first, but it kept building. Like he was pressing the edge of a long blade against my flesh, just pressing down harder and harder until it started cutting in. Whatever interest I might have felt at the start was obliterated by a sense of obscene damage, a sickness, that went right to my stomach. I laughed because I couldn't believe how much it hurt. It seemed like a bad joke. Because I'd laughed, he caned me again, harder. This time I cried out, in anger more than anything else. I thought he would realise I wasn't into it, and stop, but he kept going. I held out as long as I could. Then I said the safe word: 'unicorn'.

It stunned him. Claire had said her tattoo was a silly youthful identification with New Age sensibilities — but it wasn't, or it wasn't only that. It was a marker of an unwise period of her life. He felt certain that the safe word in this encounter had been her choice. Perhaps she had used *unicorn* with every dominant man she met; had insisted upon it, like a calling card. Perhaps he'd had a special name he wanted her to call him, too; David imagined the two of them behaving like children with secret identities in a playground game that wasn't a game, that was terrible and serious. He'd found a caning scene online when he was researching the questions Claire had presented, and had hardly been able to watch, it progressed with such horrible speed: a bruise, a welt rising, the skin whitening as after a bad burn, and then the first trickle of blood ... That was what Claire had exposed herself to. One flimsy little safe word between her and irreparable damage. Who *was* this person whose name she couldn't remember? What if he'd ignored her and carried on?

Tattoos were symbolic, everyone knew that. He'd always found Claire's choice of symbol baffling, naive, even more so once he discovered how much trouble she took to conceal it. Why keep this thing that you were no longer proud to display? She plastered it over with Dermablend whenever she went bare-legged. Why not get rid of it altogether? They could do that now. They could laser it away. But he'd always had the horrible idea that the tattoo was somehow more permanent than he was; that he would be lasered away first.

C. was a doctor at a hospital in Leeds. That was where we went — never his house, just an on-call room with a single bed, a lockable door. He was very handsome: tall and solid, green eyes, Hollywood nose. Too handsome for the site I'd found him on. He knew it, too. But he had appetites ordinary beautiful girls wouldn't indulge. I pinned a lot of hope on him, despite his clarity about the fact that I was not his girlfriend. I desired him very deeply. Sometimes he was so exhausted he'd fall asleep after half an hour, and I'd lie beside him tormented with longing. Once we went to a

kink night together, and as he steered me through the half-empty
rooms he said, You're the prettiest girl here, not that there's much
competition. He never came with me until the last time we saw
each other, when he tied my wrists and ankles together then got
me to kneel on the bed. He wasn't wearing a condom. I wasn't on
the pill, but I thought he knew that. I thought he'd pull out. He
didn't. I had to ask him for a morning-after pill. He was a doctor,
after all. We were in a hospital. He looked at me closely, and I
knew he was realising things about me – that I was irresponsible
with my body in ways that were not convenient to him; that I
could not be trusted. It doesn't work like that, he said.

She had told him before about getting called the prettiest
girl in the club, but not what kind of club this had been. The
comment had amazed Claire with its cruelty. It hadn't amazed
him. Masses of men out there would casually humiliate and
then discard a woman like Claire. David knew this because
he had been one of those men once: he had started sleeping
with a girl for whom he did not care, and found that he was
angered by her needs, by the indifference she revealed in him,
as if she were a mirror that showed his ugliest face. What had
made him angriest of all had been this girl – Samantha – this
girl Samantha's exponential desire to please, which grew more
craven the crueller he was. Clearly Claire also had the capacity to displace her own needs entirely in favour of someone
else's, to empty herself, to make herself a receptacle for some
unworthy overbearing personality to pour itself into.

Had Claire been able to consider this tendency, or
any other tendency, in her notebook entries, she might

have been on to something. But each of her experiences floated alone in the otherwise empty tank of a page, without context. The notebook's lack of reflection was beginning to annoy him. These were specimen jars where there should have been an ecosystem. Did she *think* while she was writing? Or did she just set things down, drawing no conclusions, joining nothing up, emptying herself with no consequence, not even the penance of confession? It was a misogynistic trope, he knew, to imagine that a woman didn't think; and he could not exactly say that there was no evidence of thought in the notebook's words. The commitment of these memories to paper was an act of recollection. Some of the accounts were sensitively written. But where was the thinking-*through*?

He, as her partner, could fill in the blanks. He could recall the agonised conversations about the lies she had told him, the period of time in which she had, with painful hostility, surrendered the image she had constructed of herself as a willing submissive, admitting finally that she was no longer interested in being restrained or choked, and perhaps had never been truly interested in the first place ('interested' being her word for 'aroused'). On their first holiday together, they had checked into a cheap hotel in Madrid to discover that their room contained an iron four-poster bed. Seeing this contraption, David had thought to himself that perhaps now, abroad, would be a good time to relax his principled stance enough to try tying Claire up. She had looked startled when he suggested it; then she had acquiesced, allowing him to knot her wrists and ankles to the corners of the frame with straps from their luggage; and he had gone down on her, nestled between her spread legs, and done his best to please her, until she had fallen very quiet and he had looked up to find her in tears.

He knew this; he could join the dots; but what if a stranger read the notebook? What would they make of it? Of her? There was little chance of anyone getting their hands on the notebook: the space beneath the mattress, the privacy of the flat, the analogue nature of the notebook itself, were precautions against exposure. Precautions — but not a guarantee. And then there was the greater risk the notebook ran, the risk run by anything recorded anywhere, in any fixed, observable form, which was epistemological. To set these encounters down was to accept them as knowledge. Wasn't there something obscene about this, separate from the obscenities the notebook described? It made him want to take the book down to the beach and burn it.

He didn't, of course. He had returned to the end of the entries, which were rapidly approaching the end of the book. He put it back.

Caro came for dinner. David had to clear all his paperwork off the dining room table. She arrived with her wide eyes and her fake fur coat, carrying a bottle of syrupy dessert wine — who drinks dessert wine? — in a paper bag. She wouldn't sit down, but hovered, examining bookshelves, pulling things off, going, 'Have you read this? Have you read this? Is it any good?' Claire flurried and crashed in the kitchen. She was roasting a rack of lamb, which she'd never done before: she'd had to buy a roasting tin. He and Caro were alone in the living room.

'Why don't you sit down?' he asked, handing her a glass of red wine.

'Oh God, no, I've been sitting down all day. So Claire is really lonely,' Caro said, a monstrous change of gears. 'Are you lonely too?'

Her pupils were enormous, her irises witchy green.

'Not at all,' he said, determined not to give her the smallest satisfaction. Let her think he'd known Claire was lonely (had he known? was it even true?) – that there were no secrets between them. 'But what about you? It's hard to be new in town.'

'Oh, I never get lonely,' Caro said. 'I just get bored.'

'You must be bored, then. After *London*.'

'God no. This place is incredible. The English department – it's like the 60s didn't happen up here, you know? It's like post-structuralism just completely passed them by.'

David could not prevent himself from saying, 'I'm sure that's not true.'

'They haven't even got round to postcolonialism yet, never mind decolonial literature. Oh, it's true. Believe me. They're absolutely resistant to it. It's a real old boys' club. Totally reactionary. It's kind of amazing, really. I didn't think anything like this had survived the 90s. And the chauvinism! I speak in meetings and they look at each other like, what the fuck?'

David doubted this too. His experience of female colleagues speaking in meetings was that their suggestions were politely tolerated, then quietly, later, ignored. But he just kept sipping his wine.

'And nobody's having sex up here,' she said, making him jump. 'What's up with that? None of the post-docs are even socialising, let alone fucking.'

She was staring at him pointedly as she said this. The inner rims of her lips were darkly stained from the wine. He felt an angry sweat break out beneath his arms.

'How do you know?'

'You can tell. Everyone's all pinched and closed in on themselves. Maybe they're falling in love. Is that it? Maybe everyone's just secretly falling in love with each other but never doing anything about it. Ugh! What a waste of time.'

'How is that a waste of time?'

'Because love and sex, they're not separate things,' Caro said unblinkingly. 'You can't treat them like that. Thought is made in the mouth. Love is made in the cunt.'

He couldn't help it: he blushed, and Caro saw it, and gave a small smile of satisfaction. Did she say 'cunt' around Claire? He bet she did. He bet Claire let her. Of course he knew it must be a different experience altogether to be a woman and to hear another woman use the word than it was to be a woman and to hear a man use it. Moreover he knew that new friendships demanded particular kinds of politeness and receptivity. But he still felt hurt. There was one rule for Caro and another for him.

She roved off again, glass slopping in her hand, and went behind the sofa to the window, where the deep white windowsill held a crispy spider plant, a couple of singed candles, and a picture of David and Claire in a heavily textured metal frame.

'Where's this?' she asked, picking the frame up. 'God, she looks so young.'

'Conference in Vancouver. We went together.'

'You were both giving papers?'

'No, just me.'

'That was good of her.' She took a swig at her wine. Held the picture at arm's length. 'So what was your paper about?'

This he could answer very smartly. 'Institutional exposure in policy determination.'

Caro pulled an awful face. 'Insta *what*?'

'Institutional exposure, legal exposure, in policy determination. Say you've got a—'

'Hang on, hang on. I thought you were both philosophers?'

'We are.'

'Then why are you talking HR bollocks?'

'Caro,' he said, his laugh tight, 'what do you think we do? Do you think we just sit around discussing the existence of God?'

'That's what Claire's doing.'

'No, it isn't.'

'Of course it is. Lady Mary Shepherd. David Hume. Prime mover and all that. She seems to think about God a *lot*.'

'She thinks about *Shepherd* a lot.'

'And Shepherd thought about God.'

There was a long pause, in which the background clatter from the kitchen separated out once again into its component parts: a knife stuttering on a chopping board, plates clacking in the sink. Eventually Caro tipped her head to one side. 'Do you think she needs a hand?'

He did not realise he had been waiting for it until it finally appeared: an entry about the teacher.

Claire had told David about the teacher long ago, when they were first going out: not privately, not soberly even, but in the Lachlan Hotel bar with a whole group of other philosophers – Bradley the Californian was there, Melissa maybe – back when they were all still doctoral students. This was following a guest lecture on criminality, after which they had started talking about their own youthful indiscretions. How criminal were *you*? Claire had not led with the story of the teacher, but with the confession that in her teenage years she had been so good at hiding Body Shop products up her sleeves that she had taken orders from her friends.

'Oh, shoplifting,' Bradley said, 'we've all done that. The real question is, how much did you ever lift in one go? I once got a twelve-pack of Bud and a dozen glazed doughnuts out of a Costco.'

Claire had laughed like everyone else, but David had felt her tense beside him. She found Bradley abrasive sometimes, attention-hogging. He'd thought it was that. But in fact she was tense with adrenaline, steeling herself. The laughter died down, and she blurted out: 'When I was sixteen, I had an affair with one of my teachers.'

A shocked pause, even Bradley falling quiet for a moment, before his motor started running again.

'You know,' he said, 'it's amazing how many people own up to things like that. It's like there must be affairs happening in every single school. Was he married?'

'Married? No. He was only ten years older than me.'

'That's not so bad. At least he wasn't one of those creepy-ass fifty-year-olds with a Peter Pan complex.'

David's mind had thrummed with questions too, but he hadn't felt able to ask them, not publicly. Instead he'd sat there as if he already knew all about it, willing Claire to look at him across the foamy rims of the pint glasses. Eventually, she did: a darting look, nervously defiant.

'What was the sex like?' Melissa asked.

Claire shook her head. 'We never had sex. We just messed around for a few weeks. Then he left to teach abroad.'

'Dude,' Bradley said, 'that's not an *affair*. You can't use the word *affair* if he never actually fucked you.'

Walking home along the burn, back to Claire's rented room, David had said, 'Was that true? About the teacher?'

It wasn't the right approach – he knew that immediately. She'd turned to him, vulnerable, defensive, and said, 'Why would I make that up?'

'No, not that you'd ... I just thought, those kinds of conversations. You exaggerate things sometimes. I know I do.'

She frowned. 'I think, if I was going to exaggerate, I would've said we *did* have sex. We really didn't. We had nowhere to go – you know, to be private. And we talked a lot. It was all very chaste.'

'I wish you'd told me first.'

'I didn't think of it. I forget about it all the time. It really wasn't a big deal.'

'OK.'

'So that's all right? It doesn't bother you?'

What could he have said? That she was the one who needed to consider the question of bother? That she was setting him a trap, forcing him to say it didn't bother him simply because she claimed it didn't bother her? But those had been the early days, when he had not yet found the footing from which to challenge her sense of the world. He had mainly wanted to get her back to her room, out of her clothes.

It began on a school ski trip to France when I was sixteen. T. was twenty-six. All the sixth-formers were allowed to stay up drinking in the hotel bar with the teachers in the evenings, and T. and I talked a lot, longer and longer each night as the week progressed. He was young, he was handsome and lively, all the other girls fancied him too, but he wanted to talk to me. We were staying up till midnight, one o'clock. I can't remember what the conversations were about now. I just remember the feeling of blossoming under his attention like a dried flower in a glass of warm water. Eventually, on the last night, when we were the last two people in the bar, he put his arms around me and said, in a bewildered sort of way, What are we doing? I didn't dare move in case he took his arms away. Back in England, we began to meet up, a couple of evenings a week, at pubs on the other side of the city. When the pubs kicked out we would walk in the woods. We held one another. We talked. We kissed.

Sometimes we lay down, if we could find a spot where that was possible, but we never undressed: the most I experienced of his body was his hot stomach and the small of his back when my hands could find their way beneath his shirt. It was the same with me: little portions of my skin were on offer, but nothing more. Sometimes he touched my breasts through my clothes. Sometimes I felt the lump in his jeans press against me, but I never touched him there and he never encouraged me to. In the whole time we were seeing each other, which lasted about five months, we had one full night together, when we went away for the weekend, Saturday to Sunday, to the Lakes, to a B&B. My parents knew – in a fit of guilt I'd told them – and once the storm blew over my mother at my request had taken me to buy a new bra and knickers. The ones I chose were lace and satin in an oxblood colour. In the bedroom of the B&B, T. saw the strap of the bra poking out of my T-shirt, and he touched it and said, What's this?, because in all our time together he had never glimpsed a strap that colour. I felt embarrassed, like I had been caught out in a lie, pretending to be someone I wasn't. The room was cold and quiet. It was unspoken between us that we were going to have sex that night. I was afraid. I think he was too. We dropped our bags and went to the pub instead. We picked at some food. We got a bit drunk. Then we went back to the room early and undressed one another very shyly and stood there kissing, holding one another. He kept sighing, as if he was sad. Eventually we moved to the bed. I was trying to do the right thing. I went down on him for a while, the first time I'd ever done it, just sucking instead of moving my head up and down. Eventually he drew me back up towards him. He put a condom on. He got on top of me, and tried to enter me, but he couldn't. He wasn't hard enough. I tried touching him through the condom but that just seemed to make things worse. He rolled away. He said, I'm sorry, C (he called me C). I said it was fine, it was fine. I wanted above all to be reassuring. Perhaps I had read about this in a magazine – the need to minimise pressure on 'your man'. We cuddled for a while. Soon he fell asleep, but I'd never shared a bed with anyone before. I lay awake for hours, tingling with nearness, trying not to move, not to breathe. We spent the next day looking around the town, holding hands, enjoying our anonymity this far from home. We kissed by the lake. We never mentioned what had happened in the night. Then he drove us back in the afternoon and dropped me at my parents' house. I walked in proudly, displaying myself to them as a girl who was old enough to make her own decisions, to get herself back in one piece.

That was her first time: not the Novotel with M. That was it. The scumbag teacher. Her first one. David thought again of the way she had told this story, as a colourful harmless episode, something to brandish in the pub, to trump a competitive interlocutor, produced from her sleeve like one of the Body Shop lipsticks her so-called friends had commissioned her to steal. Oh, no, they'd never had sex. It was all so chaste. At pains to impress this upon him. She had convinced herself that losing your virginity was nothing but the simple mechanical act of admitting a penis into your vagina, which allowed her to believe that she had not lost it to the teacher. No wonder her first time hadn't felt like an event! *That* had been the event: the first total nakedness, the first mutual willingness to do anything, do it all, successfully or not ... But she'd told herself it wasn't, on a stupid technicality, all this time.

What toll had it taken on her, the teacher's failure to see it through? She must have blamed herself. Even twenty years later, writing this entry, she was determined to describe her own sexual inadequacy – that she hadn't known how to give a blowjob – without considering his. She probably still thought she'd done something wrong. Scumbag cunt. Not even to talk about it with her! Not to reassure her in the night! Probably the teacher couldn't get it up because he was afraid of what he was doing. Had this occurred to Claire? That he knew it was wrong? Or maybe it was a chronic problem for him. Maybe he was so fucking inadequate he couldn't keep it up with anyone at all, and he'd thought sleeping with someone inexperienced was the only way to get through it. Maybe the new bra made her look too grown-up.

David could hardly begin to consider the implications of Claire's mother taking her to buy underwear for this outing. He'd never liked Anne, though it was not unusual to dislike one's in-law; but this new information made him dizzy. Almost euphoric. Not only had Anne known that her daughter was being abused, not only had she allowed her abuser to take her away for the weekend, but she had bought her daughter lace and satin underwear for this assignation, like a brothel madam taking her newest acquisition to the lingerie shop. Now he could not picture the scene – Claire and the teacher in bed – without also picturing Anne there too, standing by the window in her shiny apron, waiting to clean up the mess.

He had a sudden sickening conviction that Claire would have told this story to Caro, and that Caro would have affirmed all the worst aspects of Claire's telling – would have said stupid things about sexuality being weirder than convention allows, about girls all maturing at different rates, about how loads of her friends slept with their teachers and they're all fine, are liberated even, what passes for liberated in Caro's world, piercing their tongues and making shit art and living in London like rats. She would have told Claire that the narrative of the critical event in one's past, the event from which all future unhappiness stems, is a Freudian construct that denies the complexities, the errancies, of human development, perceived time. Far from being reassuring, this would only have thrown Claire into further confusion. Was her mother really wise and enlightened? Was her past not really that bad?

He listened to Claire clumping away down the street until he couldn't hear her any more, until he was fully alone with himself, and all the charged particles of anger began to fall and settle on the chairs, the table. He went to the bedroom and stripped the bed, pummelling the duvet, bundling the greasy sheets together then throwing them, hard, like a medicine ball, into the corner of the room. He knew he'd mishandled the situation. He'd admitted as much to Claire, but by then she was too far gone, too sunk in her bath of self-pity, to hear him.

It had begun that afternoon, when he'd suggested a walk up the coast. They hadn't done anything like it all winter, but now the light was coming back, the daffodils were poking up, and he'd felt a need to escape the confines of the flat, which still seemed to harbour a faint smell of fatty lamb from the meal with Caro. In the back of his mind lay an unexamined plan to draw Claire out of her usual surroundings in order to draw her out of herself, allowing her to talk about subjects that were otherwise disbarred – the teacher, he'd hoped, and even, with luck, her mother.

It was a bright, cold, windy afternoon. Claire's hair had been loose – she had not thought to bring a bobble – and when they got down on to the sands, the wind had whipped it around, the strands catching in her mouth, her eyes. People brought their dogs here to watch them race towards the horizon, ears flying, in pursuit of flung toys. A greyhound in a little red jacket, head down, had sprinted up to Claire, sniffed her crotch, then leapt away. She'd looked embarrassed, as if the dog had sensed something about her in particular, a distinctive, distracting smell.

The sands curved north, the low tide glittering in the distance, and they'd followed the curve towards the headland, not talking much, their hands deep in their pockets, looking around. The further they'd got from town, the fewer people they had seen, though the occasional thwack of a golf ball or wind-torn shout reached them from the links to their left. He had felt his ears burn with cold, and wondered if they'd have to go much further. Beyond the headland, across the wide mouth of the estuary, lay the nature reserve, which was another broad sandy beach, but this time with visible sandbars shoaling out into the water, where the seals came to calf.

He'd thought he would begin by saying something about one of his female students, who had recently sent him an email signed with an X, a kiss. He'd thought he would say how uncomfortable this made him, which would allow him to get Claire talking about inappropriate communications between lecturers and undergraduates, a topic that was only a hop and a skip away from her and the teacher. But she had derailed him by speaking first.

'I think it's finished,' she'd said.

A moment of blind desolation overtook him, before he realised that she was talking about her book.

'Really?'

'Yes, *really*,' she'd said, as if he'd implied – perhaps he had – that she might be mistaken. 'I mean, I need to check the index one more time. But basically it's done.'

That would have been the moment to congratulate her, supplying, as he was expected to supply, the requisite excitement. But her readiness to read criticism into even the most innocuous response had annoyed him, so he'd only asked, 'How do you feel?'

'I don't know,' she'd said. 'It's ... weird.'

They had reached the end of the sandy stretch, where the steep spine of headland broke up through the beach and jagged off into the sea. The little cliff path with its faded wooden signpost twisted away through the heather. Claire had set off ahead of him. Before he could stop himself (though why should he have stopped himself?), he'd told her not to climb with her hands in her pockets. She snorted over her shoulder, said she wasn't going to slip, and he'd replied that nobody ever *knows* they're going to slip, and could she just take them out, all right? She had continued walking ahead of him, her back stiff; then she had removed her hands from her pockets and held them out at her sides, exaggeratedly, as if she were crossing a beam.

They'd reached the crest of the headland, emerging in the rough beyond a green. The wind had been even stronger up there, tugging madly at their clothes. They'd paused to look at the view, or pretended to, at least: he'd had the feeling that they were both trying to drum up some kind of response to the glittering expanses of sea before them, though Claire would never have admitted it, standing there with her hair flattened against one side of her head and ballooning out on the other. He wouldn't have admitted it either. He would have stayed as long as she wanted to, gazing out towards where Kristiansand would be, if you sailed far enough. He'd wondered whether she was doing this on purpose: making him stand there feeling nothing as a way of answering the question he had asked. But that was crazy. She didn't *know* he was feeling nothing.

She'd turned to face him then. The clarity with which he'd seen her, in the unflinching spring light, was extraordinary – the reddened tip of her nose, the little gleam of wetness on the rim of her nostril, the bluish line at her temple, the glint of down on the curve of her upper lip, not quite a moustache, but not insignificant either – and he became conscious that he, too, must be just as clearly illuminated, all his pores and crevices and hairs revealed, all the incipient decrepitudes of middle age. They were both at the point, physically, where their twenties were finally behind them for ever; the point from which there was no turning back. He saw it in the coarsened texture of Claire's pale chin.

Then the idea had come to him that Claire was about to say that she *knew* he had read her notebook, had known all along, had after all been writing it for him, for him to find, setting down the things she could not bring herself to say. It seemed impossible, suddenly, that this was not the case. How could two people face each other as closely, as candidly, as this, in the floodlights of March, and not know all there was to know about one another? She must see him already; she must have worked him out and found him wanting, but sat on the knowledge until her monograph was complete, until she had no use for him, could free herself at last ...

'How's *your* book going?' she asked.

In a blink – one blink of hers: he saw her take it – the fancy had left him. Of course she didn't know. She didn't even know how she felt about her own first significant scholarly achievement. He'd felt relief at this, but it possessed a deflated quality, as if it had come at the expense of a buoyancy that might have lifted them up and off the cliff together, floating out over the mouth of the river, over the sandbars, the basking seals.

By asking him about his book, she was embarking upon one of her most familiar offensives. He had recognised it immediately. She was exercising her right, now that she had at long last finished her own work, to nag him about his; and if he refused to be nagged, if he was grumpy about it, then she would exercise her right to intervene in that very grumpiness, to try and shame him out of it, the way he had tried to shame her out of her own procrastination. Seeing this, he had refused to answer, and they had turned back and retraced their steps in silence, each dwelling on the hurt they had sustained, a terrible pressure growing between them. As soon as they reached the flat, she had gone straight to the bathroom for a handful of tissues and blown her nose. Then, still clutching the tissues as if they were a crumpled flower, she had appeared in the living room doorway and said, 'Why can't you just be happy for me?'

Why not indeed? Hadn't he been begging her for months, for years, to finish the book? It was natural for her to expect him to be glad when it finally happened. But her book – the need for her to finish her book – had been a mainstay of almost their whole relationship, a project that they were in some sense engaged to execute together. Wasn't it also natural for him to feel bereft?

Too late, he'd said, 'Why don't we go out for dinner? To celebrate?'

'I can't,' she'd said, with furious satisfaction.

'Why not?' he'd asked, stupidly, then knew. What else would she be doing? 'You're going to see Caro. Of course you are.'

And then he felt sorry – foolish, even – for not making more of a fuss, because he knew that Caro was going to do exactly that, especially if she learned that David had failed to rise to the occasion. He pictured the two women, without him, lifting giddy glasses of champagne, toasting his absence as much as Claire's success.

'Cancel,' he'd said, 'cancel and come with me.'

But he knew it was pointless, and this sense of pointlessness made its way into his voice, enfeebling what should have been a heartfelt request, so that Claire was perhaps justified in looking at him as scornfully as she did, and saying, he thought quite nastily, 'Why would I want to do that?'

She'd left, early, in her clumpy boots and a shirt he'd never seen before, the same colour as the notebook's cover. He'd almost commented on the match, then caught himself, then caught himself again – what did it matter? She'd never hidden the notebook's existence from him. She knew he'd seen it in her hands. But by then it had been too late: the latch had fallen behind her, the flat had begun to hum with emptiness, and he'd gone to the bed and stripped it as if he had caught her with someone else.

He looked at the mattress's grid of squashy diamonds, satiny and synthetic, the stains here and there that he wanted to think were coffee. Unlike the rest of the furniture, the bed did not belong to the landlord. It was Claire's. He'd never been sure how he felt about that. Was sleeping on a stranger's mattress, where untold numbers of other strangers had previously had sex, any worse than sleeping on the mattress upon which your own girlfriend had fucked dozens of other men before she met you?

He ferreted the notebook out.

B. was a virgin. He came to my room in halls one night and we discussed it and in the process of the discussion he told me that he would like his first time to be with me, so I obliged. We put the lamp on. We went to bed. He was smiling, but not to cover up his nervousness — it was a kind, honest smile that acknowledged his anxiety and his own amusement at himself. He was a very calm presence although he trembled. The skin of his chest was brown and soft, his nipples very plump, and his penis was large — too large, almost, improbably mismatched to his gentleness. He didn't know what to do with it. On one level I liked the feeling that I did know what I was doing — I liked the power, the confidence, it gave me. On another level I felt closed out of my own experience, but this time by the power I held, not by the power I was lacking. Afterwards he was plainly grateful but also, I suspect now, probably disappointed, and perhaps even hurt by the whole thing, while I made crude comments to myself like 'I've deflowered a virgin!', enjoying the illusion that I'd done this sensitively, when of course I had deprived him of the chance I'd had myself: to do it for the first time with someone who loved him.

He felt hot: scorched, almost, as if he'd looked down into a smoking pan. 'Monstrous' did not seem too strong a word. It was monstrous to acquiesce to someone's wishes like that, knowing what you knew, knowing that they would regret it. Monstrous to crow about it afterwards. Almost *more* monstrous to write it down so frankly; to be able to see so clearly what you had done wrong. She'd used this B., not for sex, but for the experience of being in control: to see how it felt. She'd stolen something from him that he'd never get back. It was not dissimilar to what the teacher had stolen from her. So she hadn't only learned abjection from her earlier life. She'd learned manipulation too.

He returned, he could not help it, to the part about B.'s penis, its being improbably large. Improbable compared to what? To whose? He thought of the Soho sex shop where they had bought Claire's vibrator; of the display of toys, mounted and lit like a seventeenth-century armoury. Claire had pointed to one of the dildos, half-laughing, and said, 'My God, that's *huge*', and a thrill of angry embarrassment had run through him. What she'd said was true: the navy blue dildo was ridiculously, injuriously huge, clearly a fantasy object. But the comment, made carelessly in public, had bothered him nonetheless. It bothered him that it bothered him, and silently he had blamed Claire for this too: for revealing in him a weakness.

He opened the bedside cabinet and took the vibrator out. A thin layer of dust clung to the tacky surface. Behind the vibrator lay a pack of wet wipes in individual sachets, like the sort they dispense on planes after a meal. Almost none of them had been used. He took out one of the wipes – a strong scent of lemons rose from its wetness – and used it to clean the vibrator off. The purple surface glistened; there were depths to it, artificial ones, jewelled somehow. The texture reminded him of the rubbery bouncing balls he'd liked when he was a child.

He switched it on. It shuddered in his hands; the shining bunny-ears shook. Monstrous, too. What a monstrous invention. He knew it wasn't liberal to think so, but in the moment he did not care. A fury overtook him. He got hold of the vibrator with both hands and began to try and break the shaft in half, as if it were one of those glow-sticks you have to crack to let the light out. Even as he did this, he knew how absurd it was, how pathetically symbolic – but he seemed to know all of it, to be removed so many times from himself that none of the frames would hold, and so he was delivered back to the petty but entirely satisfactory violence he was committing none the wiser, with the shaft bending in his hands: bending, but refusing to break. He had to tuck the ball-end of it, the battery pack, into his armpit to get the leverage. Then it began to give. Not with a theatrical snap, of course – he should not have expected the satisfaction of that – but with a slow, silent disjointing of whatever gave it structure inside its rubber sleeve. The sleeve held the parts in place. You couldn't even tell it was damaged unless you applied some pressure. He laughed with the broken thing in his hands. Then he put it back where he had found it, and returned the notebook to its hiding place as well.

He found clean sheets in the chest of drawers. He made the bed, got into it deliberately early. Let her come home to a dark flat. He read for a respectable fifteen minutes, then switched off the lamp. He thought it might be hard to fall asleep, but it wasn't. He dreamed that a student came to his office and asked him what it meant, and when he asked what what meant, she said, last night, when we were together; but he had no memory of what she was suggesting, he wouldn't have done that, why would he have done that, when she wasn't even objectively very attractive? So he tried to tell her that it had never happened, or that it could never happen again, and to persuade her to keep it to herself, but she started crying so loudly that all his colleagues left their offices and came along the corridor to investigate. He could literally see them putting it together as they rallied around the girl, giving her their jackets to wear, putting their arms around her and making her sit on their laps, all the time glaring at David. The hostility in the room was incredible. He was sweating. He could hardly move. He was filled with a sense of absolute dread that he had completely fucked everything up, everything – Claire, the job, his whole career – for this stupid crying girl whom he didn't even like. Even as she sat on his colleague's bony knees, she kept reaching out to him, and there was something in her hand . . .

The sound of Claire scrabbling to fit her keys in the door woke him. He lay there, groggy and sour, and listened to her banging around, running the taps, getting ready for bed. She put the hall light off before she opened the bedroom door, so it wouldn't disturb him; but she didn't come into the room right away. She stood there, in the doorway, not looking at him exactly – it was too dark for that – but sensing him somehow, testing the tautness of the air, to tell if he was awake; if he would speak. Sometimes they reconciled like this, late at night, in the darkness, holding one another affectionately, relaxing out of their mutual tension into the weight of sleep, with only a murmured *sorry* or two. Not tonight. Even when she crept into bed beside him and placed a warm hand on his side, even when he felt the softness of her breasts against his back (was she wearing nothing at all for once?), he did not move. Her hand crept lower, seeking the point of his hip, the crease of his groin ... What was she thinking? It was painful, bewildering, that she would choose this moment, when they were hardly speaking to each other, to initiate sex. She must be properly pissed: he could smell the hoppy fumes coming off her, because of course she had only drunk beer with Caro, not champagne. Had Caro put her up to this? Had they discussed the argument? Had Caro advised Claire to go home and shag him and make up her mind?

Fuck Caro, he thought viciously. He twisted away from Claire's touch and ripped back the warmth of the duvet, making her gasp. He got up.

'Don't,' she said. 'I *want* to ...'

An odd thrill it gave him, to hear some kind of need in her voice. Of course the need was not sexual. Reassurance: that was all she wanted. A chance to make amends for how she had treated him before, going off with Caro, gossiping perhaps. Drink had made her sentimental enough to offer what she thought he wanted. But she was wrong, wasn't she? He didn't want this: drunk sex with no talking, during which she would probably – also because of the beer – begin to cry, and which stood no chance of giving her pleasure, because, as she'd told him endlessly, alcohol dulled her nerves. She was crying now. The wet snuffling sounds had begun. He didn't care. Let her cry about rejection for once, instead of crying because he'd made her reject *him*.

It was a more honest kind of sorrow. It might even do her some good.

April came; May with its foamy blossoms. They had not slept together now for almost five months, but lately it had been as much his decision as hers. Sitting in the ugly winged armchair, in the silence of the empty flat, he asked himself: am I strategising? Am I deliberately withholding my desire in a bid to make her come to me? He looked inwards, but found no desire to withhold. The urgency had gone. It ought to have worried him. Was this the onset of depression? He'd always associated the loss of sexual pressure with depression, but he could not say that he was especially depressed. If anything, life had been easier for the past few weeks. Both he and Claire had felt more even-keeled. Even hearing of Caro's antics had needled him less. And though he was not purposely trying to provoke it, Claire had been inching towards him again, touching his arm more often, even hugging him from behind when he was washing up, as he'd used to hug her.

She was never going to write about him in the notebook. He saw that now. He would never be inducted into her hall of fame – not while they were still together. Some notion of propriety endured; something, at least, resisted exposure. But did her refusal to write about him mean she would never gain perspective on their life together? Never be able to view David as directly, as honestly, as the rest? If not, what hope did they have?

Right now she was meeting her mentor in the department, to discuss what her next research project would be now that

Lady Mary Shepherd was done. He had prepared her for it thoroughly, had sent her off as determined as she got. After that, she was going to Caro's to help her write an application for a visiting fellowship. The afternoon opened up in front of him, hours in which to read the notebook at his leisure. But he felt, for the first time, misgivings; not enough to prevent him from looking, just enough to cause some delay. A bar of pale sun had fallen through the window. He watched it creep across the carpet, showing the crumbs. There hadn't been any direct sunlight in that room for months. The days were lengthening. The summer would begin — what passed for a summer this far north, endless light and little heat.

He rose sluggishly and went to the bedroom and got down beside the bed. He pushed his hand under the mattress. For a moment, he thought the notebook wasn't there. Was that — was he *glad*? Far away, his fingertips grazed the edge. He pulled back. It could have been one of the buttons that studded the mattress. A protruding spring. Could he convince himself of that?

He could not. He drove his hand deeper and grasped the notebook firmly and pulled it out. He turned to the end.

Once in Montreal I seduced a woman. She was French-Canadian. My friend hit it off with her friend, a boy, so we were left to each other, and in my pidgin French I decided to lie. 'Je suis bi,' I said. Her face lit up. She was tiny and plump, with a long shaggy fringe that made her look like a girl I'd known at school, a bad girl, who always tried to get me into trouble. We were drunk. The four of us piled into the boy's car when the bar threw us out, and he drove us back to our hotel. I took the girl to my room. She was shy: she wouldn't take off her clothes, though I tried to persuade her. I slid my hands up underneath her shirt, whispering to her that she was pretty, 'Tu es jolie, trop jolie'. She kissed me in little pecks, like a bird with a soft beak. I could tell from the way she was breathing that she was excited. I was nervous about touching her, but it didn't matter: all she wanted to do was climb on top of me and rub herself against me through her jeans. I have no idea whether she came. I certainly didn't. We fell into a stupid drunken sleep and I felt nothing. I felt like a man.

It was not the first time he had grown hard from reading the notebook, but it was the first time his hardness had not been unwelcome. He knew he should be reflecting on what the entry meant, though God knew Claire hadn't bothered – but he could not concentrate. He was absolutely rigid. Then it was like the first time he'd hunted for the notebook and found it and known he was going to open it, known he would start reading. Just like that, he knew what he would do. He was surprised he hadn't done it sooner. He opened his jeans and pulled out his cock and began to stroke it. He read the entry again. Certain phrases detached themselves and began to throb with new meaning. He groaned. He was going to come quickly. No need to flip back to the other entries today, the one about Claire's bruised breasts, though this was another thing he knew: that the next time, or the time after that, he would. He was going to use this book. It even crossed his mind to come on its spread pages, but at the last second he turned aside and cupped himself with his hand. Not today. Perhaps never. But if this new accommodation ever became as intolerable as the last, he reserved the right to ejaculate into the notebook, then squish it shut and put it back under the mattress for Claire to find.

ACKNOWLEDGEMENTS

'Broderie Anglaise' was shortlisted for the BBC National Short Story Award in 2015 and broadcast on Radio 4. My thanks to Arts Council England for a grant. Special thanks to Leonie Rushforth, Joanna Biggs, Alba Ziegler-Bailey, Ana Fletcher, and Paul Batchelor.